Aspasia

Aspasia

A Novel of Suspense and Secrets

Florence Wetzel

© 2025 Florence Wetzel

All rights reserved.

Second edition. Originally published 2002 by Writer's Club Press as *Mrs. Papadakis and Aspasia: Two Novels*.

Any resemblance to actual people and events is purely coincidental. This is a work of fiction.

No part of this book may be reproduced or transmitted in any form or by any means, graphic, electronic, or mechanical, including photocopying, recording, taping, or by any information storage retrieval system, without the permission in writing from the author.

Cover artwork and design by Henry Chen.

NOTE: Feel free to contact the author at florencewetzel@yahoo.com.

ISBN: 9798869815095

Dedicated to every Aspasia,
past, present, and future

> Lord, you know my heart.
> I never wanted to have to kill nobody.
> But I couldn't hold out to the last, like Job.
> I had done took more than I could stand.
>
> Alice Walker
> *In Search of Our Mothers' Gardens*

Contents

Tuesday...13

Wednesday..77

Thursday..109

Sunday...117

Monday..135

Next Two Weeks..181

Monday..191

Tuesday...211

Five Months Later...215

Afterword..223

Thank You...225

Stay in Touch..227

November 1992.
A small village
in the mountains
of northeastern Crete.

Tuesday

The word for the day was "family."

I was seated on a stool in my living room, surrounded by my four students. Books and board games were scattered across the floor, and the light scent of children's sweat hung in the air. A fire crackled steadily in the stone fireplace, with two of our cats sleeping on a chair close to the heat.

People thought of Crete as a sunny place, but by late November it was cold and dark. Not as gloomy as winters in the town in upstate New York where I had grown up, but you always needed a coat, and fierce winds sometimes blew small cars off the mountainsides.

The children—Petros, Maria, Nikos, and Despina—were sitting on the couch and waiting for our next activity. We had run through our usual tasks: a Dr. Seuss book, a game where we matched cards with English words on a board, followed by off-key renditions of the alphabet song, "Row Your Boat," and "This Old Man."

For our final song, "Ring Around the Rosie," we all stood up. I hoisted the coffee table a safe distance away, then we joined hands and made a circle. For the first round, we moved and fell slowly. We gathered speed with each round, then finished up by spinning in a blur, singing so fast we were down on the floor only half a minute after starting.

Now, with flushed cheeks and some of their energy expended, the children were sitting more or less obediently. Because they were only five and six years old, I gave instructions in Greek, slipping in English words whenever possible.

"The word for the day," I announced, "is 'family.' In Greek, the word is *ikoyenia*."

"*Ikoyenia!*" Petros shouted.

"That's right. But this is English class, so let's say it together in English: family."

They tried, but they stumbled on the short "i," a sound that didn't exist in Greek. The room rang with cries of "fameelee," so I had them repeat the word after me, patiently honing their vowels into something resembling English.

After each child had uttered a reasonable facsimile of the word, I praised them warmly, then brought out a drawing in a cardboard frame. The previous evening, while watching the wildly popular Greek soap opera *Lampsi*, I had drawn a picture of my family: me, my husband Dimitris, and our five-year-old daughter, Aspasia. We stood on a flower-covered mountaintop under a sunny sky, holding hands and smiling while our cats romped at our feet.

The picture was stapled into a cardboard frame decorated with dancing flowers. In the bottom part of the frame, I had written MY FAMILY in block letters.

Holding up the drawing, I said I wanted them to draw their family, namely their parents, siblings, and pets. Since almost everyone on Crete was related—as I was in fact related by marriage to all of them except Petros, who was half-Danish—I thought it better not to mention grandparents and cousins, or they would be drawing all night.

I handed out pieces of paper, assuring the children they could take more if they needed to start over.

"And when you're finished," I said, "I'll staple your drawings into the frames."

Petros didn't like this; he wanted his frame at once. So naturally the others did as well. I gave in and handed out the empty frames.

But no, they wanted the blank paper stapled into the frames. Now.

"What if you have to start your drawing over and need new paper?" I asked. "We'll have to take out all the staples."

They assured me that this would never happen.

I relented and stapled. Now each picture was so big that only two could fit on the coffee table where everyone liked to work.

Petros settled into a chair, using a large book as a drawing surface. Nikos organized himself on the floor, and the girls divided up the coffee table without much fuss. I made sure each child had a working black marker, then I put the tin with the rest of the markers on the table. As an afterthought, I propped up my drawing on a chair for reference.

"Go ahead," I said.

They began to draw.

They were my favorite class, although they required the most planning and preparation. We met on Tuesdays and Thursdays, only for an hour because they were so young. I also had three classes for older children, and in addition I tutored several students privately.

English was very important in Greece. Children used to begin learning English in junior high school, but in a recent effort to keep up with the rest of Europe, lessons now started in fourth grade.

Most children also attended the unique Greek institution known as *frondistirio*. Essentially it was mass tutoring: children attended every afternoon after they finished school, and they learned almost exactly the same material. At the high-school level, *frondistiria* covered all subjects, but younger students only studied foreign languages.

As a small village with the nearest city forty-five minutes away, we didn't have enough money for a dedicated English teacher in the grammar school, nor did we have a *frondistirio*. I was the only native speaker for miles around, which was why one of the local mothers asked me to tutor her son Giorgos.

Before I moved to Crete, I had worked as an assistant to a literary agent, which meant I had no teaching experience whatsoever. But I loved children, and I always had a soft spot for Giorgos, a gangly ten-year-old who had fallen behind in English class because he kept confusing the Greek and English alphabets.

My daughter Aspasia was a year old then. Although I was bursting with love, I was bored with repetitive tasks—nursing, burping, bathing—that required no mental agility whatsoever. Giorgos was a difficult boy, shy and stubborn, but since I had learned Greek as an adult, I knew he could learn English as a child.

Friends from America had sent me Dr. Seuss and other English children's books for Aspasia, so Giorgos and I started from the beginning with those stories. I taught him the same material as in school, but with funnier pictures and less clutter on the page. He learned the English alphabet in two weeks, and a month later he was reading simple texts.

Giorgos' progress plus a dash of Greek hyperbole gave me a reputation as the next Annie Sullivan. One day at the village store, two mothers approached me. Their children would be starting fourth grade next fall, could I start a class now so the children wouldn't struggle like Giorgos had? I agreed, which soon led to other mothers asking for more classes. Suddenly my native tongue was a pot of gold.

I taught at home, which was fine for the first few years. As my classes grew, I started to worry about not having a teaching license or insurance. Another problem was that our house didn't fit the legal definition of a safe place for children to gather, such as having two doors, a fire extinguisher, and a battery-operated exit sign.

The closest police station was three villages away, and although everyone in the nearby villages knew I taught English at home, it was unlikely the police would raid my house on their own initiative. The bigger threat came from my fellow villagers. My husband's Aunt Hara told me that I had to be careful, because someone might get jealous and report me to the police. This was a favorite pastime in Crete, where people informed on their neighbors for anything from picking a tomato off someone else's vine to having an unleashed dog. If I wasn't cautious, I might get closed down for good.

Dimitris and I discussed the situation, and we agreed that I needed my own building. But with what money? He worked as an electrician and made only enough to support us. My pay was decent, but it would be years before we had the lump sum required.

Neither of us could go to our parents for money, Dimitris because he was too proud to ask his father, and me because I barely had contact with my mother and none at all with my stepfather. We had various plots with olive trees that Dimitris had inherited, but we always swore we would never sell our land.

So that's why I had no husband then. We decided that the best way to quickly make money was for Dimitris to sign on to a cargo ship for a nine-month tour of duty. I told him he didn't have to go, but he was proud of my work and wanted me to succeed. Once Dimitris returned, I would apply for my license, then we could build a school on a piece of land we owned at the edge of the village.

I had underestimated how much I would miss him. Before Dimitris left, I was always busy with Aspasia and English classes and housework, but now that he was gone I was drowning in empty hours. When another group of mothers approached me and asked if I could start a class twice a week for small children, I said yes without hesitating.

The new class meant that Aspasia was out of the house for an extra two hours a week, but she was happy to stay with my husband's father Christos, her *papoos*. Christos was equally happy to have more time with Aspasia because he was all alone after his wife's death two years before.

So there we were.

The pictures began to take shape, but not in the way I had anticipated.

The problems began when Petros informed me that he didn't want to draw his family.

"What would you like to draw?" I asked.

"A ship."

"That's fine," I replied. "You can put your family on the deck."

"No."

"Not even as little stick figures?"

"No."

"Well—I really would like you to draw your family."

"I'll draw them at home tomorrow."

"I guess that's OK. Tell me, what are these wavy lines here on the frame?"

"Ghosts. The triangles are their eyes."

"Aha! Now I understand. Very good, Petros."

Maria had taken my instructions literally and was drawing her entire clan. She had made row upon row of circles, and she was filling them in with eyes, noses, teeth, and hair. To me they all looked alike, but Maria pointed to each face and assured me that this circle was her brother, this circle her cousin Spiros from Sitia, this one her Aunt Chrysoula, on and on through her extensive family tree.

"That's great," I told her. "But if you just draw your mommy and daddy and brothers, you'll have more room to give everyone a body with clothes."

"I don't want to do that."

"No problem," I said. "Just making a suggestion."

Nikos had grasped the assignment. His father, mother, and Despina were standing on a wavy line that was, he told me, the sea. His father was enormous and had crushed the other figures into a corner, which would have seemed odd if you didn't know their family.

I told Nikos he was doing a wonderful job, then went on to Despina. She had copied my floral frame petal for petal, and her characters were also standing on a flower-covered mountain with a friendly sun in back. However, instead of drawing her family, she had two little girls and two cats.

Crouching beside the table, I pointed to her picture. "Who are these people?"

"They're my family. It's me and Aspasia, and that's my cat Ovelix and Aspasia's cat Spike."

"It's very pretty. Maybe over here where you have some room, you could put in your mommy and daddy and Nikos?"

She looked at me as if I were crazy.

"Never mind," I laughed. "Your picture is beautiful."

I sat on the couch and watched the children while they carried on drawing. Occasionally I called out a word of praise, or handed someone a marker and asked them to name the color in English.

Glancing at the clock, I saw it was twenty minutes to six. They could draw a little longer, then I would cut up apples for their snack. Sometimes I made popcorn for them, but I was too lazy to clean out the large cooking pot, which was still full of lentils from lunchtime.

Speaking of food, what was I going to do about dinner? I could have lentils again, and Aspasia would probably eat something at her *papoos'* house. Like most Greek men, my father-in-law Christos was an excellent cook, although when his wife was alive he only stepped into the kitchen if he was in the mood.

Maybe Christos had made fish soup for supper. His soup was legendary, but then he was a legend himself. People in the village still spoke about Christos' behavior after the Chernobyl accident. When the government issued an alert against eating lettuce, Christos dismissed the warning as ridiculous. He collected lettuce from his frightened neighbors, selling the excess to travelers and making a tidy profit.

Someone coughed and broke my thoughts. Petros was standing before me, his face drawn into a tense knot. The ship wasn't working out; he now realized he had meant to draw a fire engine.

I stroked his hair and told him not to worry. We could remove the picture without ruining the frame and the ghosts.

My nails were not up to the task of taking out the staples, so I got a nail file from the bathroom. I removed the offending picture and stapled in another piece of paper. Relieved, Petros ran back to his seat to start the new drawing. I glanced at the other children to see if Petros had set off a rash of de-stapling, but they were all absorbed in their work.

Resuming my seat on the couch, I leaned back and idly ran the file over my nails. Thank God for Christos. He was always willing to babysit, which made it possible for me to teach. But Christos' helpfulness also made me feel guilty, and that's because I didn't like him. Not in the least.

I wasn't the only one who felt that way. Christos was respected in the village, but that wasn't the same as being liked. When I first moved to Crete and spoke no Greek, I thought Christos had a good sense of humor because the other men at the *kafenio* laughed at everything he said. Later I realized it was nervous laughter, the men hoping to stay on Christos' good side and avoid his caustic wit.

In time I saw the truth: Christos was the village bully. He sat in the *kafenio* day after day, legs spread wide, elbow planted on the table, surveying his domain until his gaze landed on someone or something he could criticize in his loud gravelly voice.

I also noticed that Dimitris didn't have much contact with his father. When I asked why, Dimitris said it was because he was raised by his Aunt Hara. As a child, he had run away to his aunt's house almost every day to avoid Christos' beatings, and at age six he simply stayed. His mother visited him daily, his father seldom, and after a while that was just the way it was.

As soon as Dimitris was old enough, he started working on cargo ships and was rarely home in Crete. When Dimitris settled in the village with me, he started having contact with his father again, but their relationship was always strained.

I wanted to be on good terms with Dimitris' parents, and from the beginning I had liked my mother-in-law, Pepina. A meek woman with rich brown eyes and nervous hands, she had endless patience with my broken Greek. She also taught me how to cook, clean, and sew, things I never learned from my own mother.

But Christos and I had a strange relationship, mostly due to an incident a few months after I came to the village, before I got pregnant. Pepina and I were sitting at the kitchen table, sorting out tiny stones from piles of sesame seeds. Christos roared in and demanded a cup of coffee, so Pepina scrambled to her feet and rushed to the stove. Christos dropped into the seat beside me and started complaining about the house being messy, although it was obviously clean as a church.

When Pepina set down the coffee, Christos reached out and casually smacked her on the side of the head. Dimitris had told me that Christos hit Pepina, but I had never seen it happen, and here he was striking her in front of me just as easily as swatting a fly.

I jumped up and grabbed his thick wrist. "Don't!" I shouted in Greek.

The room stopped breathing. My only thought was, "Now it's my turn," exactly as I used to think as a child when my stepfather hit my brother and then turned, ready to strike me.

But Christos didn't touch me. Instead he raised his eyebrows in surprise and laughed gruffly. I let go of his wrist and returned to my seat, keeping my eyes down as I moved the sesame seeds across the plate with trembling fingers.

From that day forward, Christos was always polite to me, or as polite as he could be to anyone. After Aspasia was born, I was beyond reproach. A male grandchild would have elevated me to sainthood, but Christos was pleased to have any grandchild at all. Dimitris' two sisters would never have children because—

Pandemonium. No good daydreaming at this job, because now Despina was under the coffee table crying, and Nikos was pummeling Petros with a pillow.

"Time for snacks!" I called out, gently taking Petros' arm and guiding him away from Nikos. "Petros, can you wash the apples for me? Find three big ones in the bowl in the kitchen."

Kneeling down by the table, I looked into Despina's tearstained face. I spoke to her quietly, coaxing out the whole horrible story. Apparently Petros had been using the light-blue marker, which Despina needed for her drawing. When he finally put the marker down, Maria snatched it, and now Despina's drawing wasn't finished.

I told Despina she could borrow the marker and finish the picture at home. This satisfied her, so I ducked into the kitchen. I sliced the apples and piled them on a plate, hurrying back to the living room before another fight broke out.

We sat on the couch, with Despina snuggled into one side of me, and Maria on the other. As we munched our apple slices, we listened to Petros describe a television show about airplanes, bits of apple flying from his mouth as he spoke.

I didn't bother with English anymore since their minds had already switched back to Greek. Oh well. I wasn't sure how much they were actually learning, but we always had a good time, despite the occasional meltdown. This group was also a nice change from my other classes, where my students were confined to chairs so they could write the letter "q" twenty times, or wrestle with verbs in a workbook.

Not that I disliked the other classes. I enjoyed them too, and I felt a responsibility to make the children's relationship with English as friendly as possible. Foreign languages were my worst subject at school, and learning Greek as an adult had been torture, at least at first. Now that I was fluent, I knew the pleasure and expanded world that a second language brings, and I wanted to give that joy to my students.

We finished the apples, then I put on my coat. The children did the same except for Nikos, who insisted he wasn't cold.

"Maybe not," I said, "but I hear there's a fine now. If you go out after six o'clock without a coat, you have to pay ten thousand drachmas."

Nikos looked at me dubiously, then picked up his coat and put it on.

I gathered the drawings, popped the last apple slice into my mouth, and raked the glowing cinders into the corner of the fireplace. The boys were already outside, running around our concrete patio. Despina and Maria waited as I shut off the lights and closed the front door behind us.

Our village was beautiful.

For centuries it had clung to the fertile green mountainsides, outlasting all the Romans, Venetians, Turks, Italians, and Germans who had passed through. Not to mention the pirates, although they never stood a chance. The village was built so it was impossible to spot from the sea, and legend had it that a lookout was posted to warn of approaching danger. By the time the pirates arrived in the village, all the humans, animals, and valuables were hidden in caves higher up. If you went to those caves today, you could still find broken pottery and animal bones.

The village overlooked a rolling valley of olive trees and nodding clover. Three mountains loomed behind us, topped with strange gray rock formations, like hot fudge sliding down ice cream. Mist filled the valley and village most mornings, and sometimes a heavy fog obscured everything, making walking difficult and flashlights useless. During those times, the village sank into a deep silence. Groping through the thick air, you might hear the click of a cane or the bleat of a goat, then the sounds dissolved into the mist.

Modern life had passed a hand over our village, but it hadn't destroyed it. When the main road to Sitia was built in the 1960s, most villages were split in half, with central squares and thousands of trees leveled in the process. A certain wholeness was lost then, and it would never come back. Luckily our village was spared: the main road simply passed us by, and even the daily buses to Sitia didn't bother to drive into the village, they just beeped from the main road.

The narrow twisting streets within the village were also intact, their large white stones smooth from centuries of foot traffic, animal as well as human. The streets were not wide enough for cars, so anyone with a vehicle instead of a donkey had to park around the village center, a circular patch of grass with a large statue commemorating the village's losses in World War II.

The village wasn't large, but it wasn't small. When I first arrived, I needed a good six months to learn all its curves and secrets. Many houses were empty, with the owners living in Athens or another big city, returning only for Easter and summer vacation. Which left a grand total of one hundred permanent residents.

People liked to ponder the fate of our village in forty years' time when all the residents over age sixty will have died out. Many believed that the young people would flee to cities or tourist resorts, and we would become another one of Crete's ghost villages. I couldn't see the future, but Dimitris and I planned to stay here the rest of our lives, and what Aspasia did was up to her. Maybe one day she'd raise her children here too.

Our home stood on the western edge of the village and was at least five hundred years old. It was a snug building with thick walls, warm in the winter and cool in the summer. Dimitris had bought the house right before I moved to the village, and it had been our home ever since.

The only downside was Mrs. Dakanalakis, a seventy-five-year-old widow who lived across the street. Although "street" wasn't quite accurate—it was more like an alleyway, five feet wide at most.

Mrs. D wasn't disabled in any visible way, yet she rarely left her home, which made my family her main source of entertainment. Only the fiercest weather or most urgent bodily functions could keep Mrs. D from her perch, a stone bench in front of her house with a direct view of our front door.

Every entrance and exit merited a comment from Mrs. D. "You're going to work early today, Dimitris" or "You look tired, Katerina! It must be from talking on the phone so late last night." Even Aspasia got grilled: "Is that a new skirt?" or "Despina hasn't been over to play recently, are you two still friends?"

Intimate questioning was a Greek personality trait I had grown accustomed to, but Mrs. D was out of control. To make matters worse, any information she extracted spread through the village at lightning speed. Villagers often stopped by to sit with Mrs. D and catch up on the latest news. Or latest rumors. Since so little happened in our village, rumors were just as good as facts. In private, Dimitris called Mrs. D "The Newspaper."

My husband was used to the lack of privacy, and because he was good-natured, he thought Mrs. D was funny. One night we were in bed about to make love, trying to be quiet since Mrs. D's bedroom was directly opposite ours. Just as I was about to insert my diaphragm, it slipped out of my hands and flew across the room. While I searched noisily in the dark, Dimitris cackled in an old lady voice, "Did you have trouble with your diaphragm again?" We laughed long and loud.

Sure enough, the next day Mrs. D asked me, "What did Dimitris say last night that was so funny?"

But I couldn't really complain about village life. We could reach the sea in twenty minutes, the small city of Sitia in forty-five. Dimitris never lacked work, and it was our very remoteness that made my teaching career possible. The local school wasn't particularly good, but we read to Aspasia every night, and when she was older we planned to take her to Athens and do civilized things like going to the cinema and eating Chinese food.

In the meantime, Aspasia was in heaven running through the village streets, loved and fussed over by everyone. She was the village's child as much as ours, which gave her an enormous sense of security.

That's not how I grew up. When I was in grammar school, we were forced to watch cautionary films about creepy men in dusty cars who approached children and asked, "Hey little girl, want a piece of candy?" Those movies terrified me, and it was a relief to know that Aspasia was untouched by this kind of fear.

One day when she and I were picking mushrooms in a shaded grove rich with the scent of oregano, Aspasia turned to me and said in her broken English, "The life is comfortable, isn't it, Mommy?"

Our village was beautiful. And the ideal place to raise a child.

"Class is over?"

Mrs. D was huddled on the bench outside her house, peering up at me from a nest of black shawls. The sun had already set, but mere cold never deterred her, especially when she knew I would be coming out with one of my classes.

"That's right," I replied as the children and I walked through the concrete patio in front of our home.

"Lots of problems today, eh? I heard the little ones fighting."

"You know how children are," I said lightly, shutting the gate behind me.

"Be careful!" Mrs. D called as I walked away. "It's dark!"

The village's few streetlamps burned out frequently and were infrequently replaced, so the children and I traveled by flashlight. I carried the drawings and the flashlight, Maria and Despina walked beside me holding hands, and the boys ran ahead.

As we walked, I tried to get the girls to say "flashlight." They knew the word "flash" from television, but the best they could manage was "flash-lie." Which was good enough for me.

We followed a twisty route through the village streets. Left at a decaying stone house nearly covered by a bougainvillea vine, right at Dimitris' cousin's house with its bright-blue wrought-iron staircase, another right at the white church. At the turn before Nikos' and Despina's house, Despina broke away and ran so she could have the honor of banging on the door.

The children's mother, a short friendly brunette in her mid-twenties, opened the door at once. She laughed as the children barreled into her, chattering about families and how Nikos hit Petros and the crisis with the light-blue marker.

"Everything OK?" she called to me over the noise.

I passed her the drawings, explaining hastily what the children had learned that day, adding that Despina had made progress with the alphabet song. The mother laughed when she saw Despina's drawing, and she laughed harder when she saw Nikos'. Immediately she promised to find a place for these new masterpieces on the already crowded walls.

She offered me coffee, even though she knew I couldn't stay—Greeks never liked to let you leave their home without consuming something. I declined, promising to come over another day. She wished me good night and shut the door.

Back on the street, Petros ran ahead and Maria slipped her hand into mine. We retraced our steps down an alleyway, then two rights and a left later we were at Maria's home.

This household was a more somber affair. The mother was in the back screaming at the two boys, and the father sat at the kitchen table with his head in his hands. He worked at the nearby gypsum mine, enduring the suffocating white dust and the constant racket of drilling. In the evenings he moonlighted, doing odd jobs like painting fences or patching up fireplaces.

We greeted each other, and he asked solemnly about our class. I told him exactly what we did, step by step. I knew this was a man with many expenses and not much money.

"And Maria drew a nice picture," I said, handing over the drawing.

Maria's small hand stayed in mine as she watched her father carefully. He smiled faintly, and immediately she dropped my hand and threw herself face down on his lap. He stroked her hair absentmindedly with one rough palm.

I said good night and went quietly out the door.

Now that we were alone, Petros took my hand. As we walked, we sang songs from class, then he sang a Danish tune in his high, sweet voice.

I asked which language he liked best, Greek, Danish or English.

"Greek," he replied. "Because it's the easiest. But English has better songs."

I told him that Aspasia felt the same way, and he asked me why she wasn't in our class. In truth I was afraid she might boss the other children, since they were in *her* house with *her* mother.

That was more information than Petros needed, so I just told him that Aspasia didn't need to attend class because I spoke English with her at home. "Like how your mother speaks Danish with you," I added.

We arrived at the village center. The two *kafenia*—one for communists and one for capitalists, with the socialists bouncing in between—were lit up and full of men. The store was also open and would be until eight. I made a mental note to go there after I dropped off Petros.

Through the window of the capitalist *kafenio*, I saw Petros' mother, Dagmar. Her thick brown hair was held back in a careless ponytail, and she was reading a book while running her fingers over the rim of a beer glass. Dagmar was an attractive woman, but the twist of bitterness in her expression diminished her charms. I could tell by her glazed eyes that she was, as usual this time of night, quite drunk.

Dagmar was in her early thirties like me, and she had arrived in the village a year before I did. She met her husband in her native land when he was working on cargo ships, just as I had met Dimitris in my country, both of us on the subway on our way to Queens.

When I first came to the village, Dagmar and I became friends, but over time she grew so dark and depressed that I found it difficult to be around her. Dagmar and her husband were genuinely in love at the beginning of their relationship, but life in the village had slowly killed her spirit.

She wasn't the first. Crete was one of the most beautiful places on earth, but it was also a rocky, desolate island that demanded a great deal of inner strength. Foreign women like me had a particularly difficult time living here. Crete's stunning nature and its notoriously handsome men had attracted us at first. But lonely winters, limited opportunities, and the claustrophobic intimacy of village life often proved too much.

I had endured my own share of hard times, but life in Crete suited me for the most part. It didn't agree with Dagmar, and on top of that she had an unhappy marriage. Her husband refused to move to Denmark, and he swore he would never let her raise the children there. Dagmar felt trapped, and like many people who saw no escape, she drank.

That was a feeling I understood all too well, since that's how I felt growing up. But I had quit drinking after graduating college, and I had a low tolerance for anyone who reminded me of my own dark days.

As I entered the *kafenio*, I glanced at the metal-rimmed clock on the wall. I decided to give Dagmar ten minutes. She only got five if I was tired, and if my mood was particularly bad, I claimed some emergency and said I had to go home at once.

I called out a general *"Kalispera sas"* to the owner and his wife, as well as the tables of card-playing men. Then Petros and I worked our way through the smoke and din to Dagmar sitting in the corner.

"Ya soo."

She looked up. "Hello, Katerina. Do you want a coffee?"

"No, thanks." A drink would make me indebted, precisely what I did not want to be.

"And here's my little Peder!" she said in her clipped, accented English. Dagmar had never bothered to learn Greek beyond a few set phrases, which surely contributed to her isolation. "How was he today?"

Petros and I both sat down, and I put his drawing on the table. "Very good. We drew pictures."

"What is this?" Dagmar declared, picking up the paper. "A fire engine! And these are—?"

"Ghosts," Petros said timidly.

Dagmar looked at me, puzzled. "But here it reads MY FAMILY."

I nodded. "That was the word for today, but we decided Petros could draw a fire engine instead." I shot him a wink, not sure how much of our English he understood.

"If the lesson was family, he must draw that, yes?" Dagmar turned to Petros. Although I knew no Danish, it was obvious she was scolding him.

"It's OK," I interrupted. "Petros plans to draw a family at home tomorrow."

"I'll have him make the drawing after school, then we'll bring it over to your house."

"No," I said slowly. "You don't understand. It doesn't really matter if Petros draws a family or not. The important thing is that he understands what the word means."

"*Ikoyenia*," Petros said quietly.

"You see? He's only five, after all."

Dagmar shook her head. "Petros needs to develop good habits. Unlike his father, who I have to tell everything at least three times before he does what I want."

I just bet you do, I thought. Glancing at the clock, I saw I had seven minutes left. "Maybe you should trust Petros a little more. He's learning quickly, much faster than the other children. But he's very sensitive."

"This is true. Petros got worried the other day when he found a photo of me and my old fiancé. I know that I told you about him, back when you still came to my house." Dagmar took a sip of beer and pursed her lips. "But you're quite busy now, aren't you? Your own little business and everything. I certainly hope no one reports you before Dimitris comes back."

I smiled, swallowing the sharp comment rising in my throat.

"Your husband is a nice man," Dagmar continued. "Good-looking too. You make each other happy, yes? And you work together as parents. Me, I am always busy trying to make my children less Greek and more Danish. Don't you feel the same with Aspasia?"

"No," I replied. "I don't."

"This is because you are American. You'll forgive me for saying so, but you have lower standards there."

Being with Dagmar always made me feel lonely, so with four minutes to spare, I pushed back my chair and said I had to go to the store before picking up Aspasia.

"We too must leave," she said. "My husband is looking after Gudrun, which means he's drinking *raki* and she's wandering around in dirty diapers."

I leaned over and kissed Petros' forehead. "Goodbye, Petros. See you on Thursday."

As I walked away from them, I wondered if I could adopt Petros. Gudrun too, for that matter.

Outside the store I saw a gray kitten, separated from its mother and living on the mean streets of our village. I had seen that kitten a dozen times in the past weeks, and I always wanted to take it home. Unfortunately Dimitris had set a firm five-cat limit right before he left.

"If they all live and sleep outside," I asked, "what's the difference?"

"Katerina," he warned. "Don't make me crazy."

I decided to ask Aunt Hara if she would take the kitten. Then I walked into the store, setting off the bells hanging on the door.

Perched behind the counter on a stool sat store proprietress Sophia Bambanakis, immaculately dressed and flawlessly made-up as always. Owner of five houses, a thousand olive trees, and several vineyards, she was the richest person in the village and glad of it. Sophia was the very definition of a big fish in a small pond. She was going to waste in our village; she should have been running the country, maybe even the world.

Sophia was also my husband's first love. They were the Romeo and Juliet of the village, madly in love but separated by her parents because Dimitris was poor and training to be an electrician. When they announced their engagement, Sophia's mother declared that she would kill herself if her daughter married a poor man with dirty hands. She even produced a knife and held it to her throat in case anyone doubted her.

Heartbroken, Sophia ended the relationship. Dimitris signed on to a cargo ship and left Crete, and Sophia married Stelios Bambanakis, older and balding, but with clean hands and plenty of olive trees. In fact, there was Stelios in the corner, measuring sugar and pouring it into small sacks.

When Dimitris brought me to the village, everyone was sure Sophia would tear me limb from limb, but she couldn't have been nicer. She was one of the few people who spoke English, and she helped me immeasurably in those early days when everything was so raw and new. I searched for glimmers of insincerity in her warm smile and manner, but since Sophia loathed almost everyone in the village and did so openly, there wasn't much chance of her pretending.

"*Ya soo*, Katerina!" She smiled and displayed her perfect white teeth, also a rarity in our village. "Is class over?"

"Yes. I just left Petros with Dagmar."

At Dagmar's name, Sophia rolled her eyes. I grinned wryly but said nothing.

"And Aspasia?" she asked. "I didn't see her today."

"It's better you didn't. Her *papoos* buys her too many sweets as it is."

"How's Dimitris?"

Sophia knew I had gotten a letter from Dimitris the previous day because the village mail was always left at her store. She took no payment for this biweekly task, but it did keep her up-to-date on everyone's business. I didn't really mind. In a village this size, privacy was a foreign concept, and personal space was a luxury belonging to no one.

I smiled at her and said, "Dimitris keeps saying he's too old to work on ships, but I can tell from his letters he's having a good time."

Sophia raised her eyebrows. "Of course! He doesn't have to worry about his wife or child, and he gets to play cards and drink all night. It's every Greek man's fantasy."

I laughed. "You're right about that."

She looked at me knowingly. "Should we start? I saved a box for you."

I was at the store for a most awkward task. Sophia knew it, and her warmth put me at ease. I nodded gratefully and said, "Let's go."

Sophia was brisk and businesslike as she loaded the box. She put in kilo bags of rice, lentils, and fava beans. Also matches, tampons, garbage bags, packages of spaghetti, dishwashing liquid, and two Break chocolate bars.

The groceries were for Dimitris' formerly crazy sister Eleni. Although I should add that the "formerly" was under dispute.

I had been in the village about a week when Dimitris asked if I wanted to meet his older sister.

"Of course," I replied. "What's she like?"

"Nice. Quiet. She a good person." We still spoke English at that point, which worked well despite Dimitris' broken grammar. "But Eleni, she used to have problem."

"What problem?"

Dimitris moved his head in a strange gesture, almost bouncing it side to side. "She a little crazy."

"In what way?"

"With her mind."

"I don't understand. Was she born that way?"

"No. But when she was teenager, she freak out. She make up crazy stories, and she start to have sex with many boys. One day she try to kill herself."

"Poor thing."

"So my father, he send Eleni to one hospital in Chania, she stay there two years. My Aunt Hara used to go see her, and one time she come back and say, 'We go next week and get Eleni, if we don't she die there.'"

"It must have been a terrible place."

Dimitris nodded. "So we bring her back, but Eleni don't want to live in the village. My uncle and me, we fix a little stone house we have in the mountains, and Eleni live there. She like it, even though they don't have no electricity."

"Did she get better?"

"Eleni take pills to be calm, I know because I buy them for her from the pharmacy in Sitia. One day she tell me, 'Dimitris, I don't want no more pills.' I say '*Ela*, Eleni, you have to take.' She tell me that for one whole year she don't take no pills, but she only say this now because she was sorry for me to spend money for nothing."

"And how is she doing these days?"

"Eleni not crazy anymore. After she stop to take the pills, she marry and everything is good. Her husband is nice man, you like him I'm sure."

We went the next day. Eleni was tall and thin with a pretty, serious face. Her husband was older with a gentle smile, and I didn't need to understand Greek to realize he had a terrible stutter.

Eleni and her husband were kind to me, and if Dimitris hadn't said anything, I never would have guessed she had such a troubled past. The only unusual thing was how quiet she was. Eleni didn't say more than three sentences the whole time we were there.

We started visiting them regularly, and I was impressed by their peaceful rural life. Eleni took care of the house, the garden, and the animals, and her husband was in charge of the olive trees, vineyards, and errands in the city. They came to the village together for holidays and parties, but whenever Christos or Pepina entered the room, Eleni and her husband—without a single word and without fuss—got up and left.

That's how it was for two years. When Aspasia was born, I started feeling differently about Eleni. I asked Pepina why Eleni hated Christos and her so much. Pepina swore Eleni's feelings had no logical basis, she was simply a violent and unstable person.

I could understand someone hating Christos, but Pepina? I started to wonder what lay behind Eleni's impenetrable quiet. I had several long talks with Pepina, who gradually convinced me that Eleni was still unpredictable and might one day harm Aspasia.

That's when I told Dimitris I wanted to limit contact between Aspasia and Eleni. He got angry, and we had an argument. I didn't win, but neither did he. Eventually Eleni learned how I felt, and my relationship with her deteriorated to the point where I stopped visiting altogether.

When Aspasia was three, Eleni's husband died. He was collecting olives outside a friend's house when he fell from the ladder, hitting his head on the concrete patio beneath the tree. Dimitris said that the hardest moment of his life was driving to the little stone house and telling Eleni the news.

From then on, Dimitris took over Eleni's olive trees, vineyards, and errands. I never helped him and he never asked me to, but when he left to work on the ship, Eleni suddenly became my responsibility. Or should I say, my burden.

"All right," Sophia declared. "That's it. When are you going, tomorrow?"

"First thing after Aspasia goes to school. Can you put this on my bill? I don't have any money on me."

"Of course."

Sophia opened the door for me as I lifted the box. She looked past me onto the street and clucked her tongue. I followed her gaze and saw, illuminated by the streetlamp, Old Manolis drunk again and swinging the gray kitten by its tail. The kitten was terrified, hissing and curling up as she tried to attack him with her claws.

I dropped the box and ran over to Old Manolis. *"Stamata!"* I cried as I hit him on the arm, my eyes filling with tears. *"Stamata!"*

He dropped the kitten and looked at me in surprise. "What's wrong?"

I called him a *malaka*—the all-purpose Greek insult, which meant "masturbator"—and marched back into the store.

There were two kinds of people in this world: those who saw something small and wanted to help it grow, and those who saw something small and wanted to exploit it for their own amusement.

"Good for you," Sophia declared. "He's the biggest *malaka* in the village."

I always believed that particular honor went to my father-in-law, but it wasn't time to argue.

"Sophia," I said. "Would you put all the groceries into bags? I'd also like to buy a yogurt, just add it to my bill."

I loaded the groceries into the trunk of my car. Ten minutes and one yogurt container later, the kitten was inside the box, howling and scratching. I thanked Sophia, picked up the box, and started walking to my father-in-law's to pick up Aspasia.

Dimitris' younger sister had problems too.

During my first year in Crete, the only thing Dimitris would say about her was "Stamatina lives in Athens." And if pressed, "She works as an interior decorator, and she's married to a lawyer."

Stamatina never came to the village, not even for our wedding. Dimitris and I had no reason to go to Athens, at least until I discovered I was pregnant and insisted on seeing an American doctor. Dimitris arranged for us to stay with a childhood friend who lived near Syntagma Square.

"What about your sister?" I asked. "Can't we stay with her?"

"Oh no," he replied. "No, no, no."

"Why not?"

"Stamatina doesn't like having people overnight. We could if we absolutely had to, but you wouldn't like it."

"How do you know?"

Dimitris made that same odd motion, bobbing his head from side to side. "She's a little strange."

Here we go again. "In what way?"

"It's hard to describe."

"Can I at least meet her?"

Dimitris grimaced. "Better not."

But I persisted, and after we went to my doctor's appointment, Dimitris phoned Stamatina. She invited us for coffee at ten the next morning.

We took a bus to Glyfada, a posh Athenian suburb. After a short walk, Dimitris stopped in front of a stately white house with gleaming black iron gates and immaculate flower beds.

"Very nice," I commented.

Dimitris grunted. He looked as if he were about to be flayed, whereas I was wearing a brand-new flowered dress and was so pregnant and happy I was practically flying.

We rang the bell. Stamatina answered at once; she must have been waiting by the door. I wanted to laugh when I saw her, because she looked just like Dimitris. Same blue-green eyes, same crooked front tooth, and same thick black hair, except hers was long and styled into a flawless bun.

Stamatina and Dimitris exchanged cheek kisses, and I watched Dimitris tense as she touched him. What on earth was his problem?

"Don't leave that there," Stamatina said to me as I was about to set my purse on the hall table. "I'll put it in the closet. You do speak Greek, don't you?"

"Now I do," I laughed, "after two years of agony. But I'm not fluent."

"Try to speak slowly," Dimitris told his sister. "You know you talk too fast, and Katerina won't be able to understand."

A short, stout man came into the foyer. He kissed Dimitris on both cheeks and shook my hand.

"Aristotelis," Dimitris said. "This is Katerina, my wife."

"A pleasure," he assured me.

We walked into the living room. I decided they must have just moved in, because the house smelled like new furniture, and there were few signs of occupancy. Everything was in the best of taste and perfectly coordinated: the couch matched the curtains and the border on the rug, and an unusual bronze metal was repeated throughout the room in ashtrays, coasters, and bookends.

They're loaded, I realized. I looked over at Aristotelis, fresh and elegant in a white shirt Dimitris only had to glance at to get dirty. Was he jealous of them? I doubted it. One of the reasons I loved Dimitris was his indifference to material things. I couldn't believe he didn't want to see his sister because he envied her ashtrays.

The men started talking about Aristotelis' law practice, and I went to the kitchen to help my long-lost sister-in-law. The kitchen was equally immaculate, like something out of a design magazine. Stamatina appeared not to have sliced a lemon or toasted a single slice of bread.

I pulled out a wicker chair with a plump strawberry-colored cushion, which matched the tablecloth and curtains. I watched as Stamatina measured coffee into a percolator, not on the stove in a *briki*, the small pot traditionally used in Greece to make coffee.

"This is a lovely house," I remarked. "How long have you lived here?"

"About eight years."

"You're joking! Everything is so clean."

Stamatina turned around and beamed at me. "Thank you. I do my best to keep it that way."

"You must have help."

"No, it's just me."

"But you work full-time! I admire you." My own housekeeping was hasty and distracted, with many things swept under the couch or dumped into closets.

"I couldn't have help," she said. "Although I'd love to. I've tried a few times, but you know how it is. I prefer things done a certain way."

Stamatina did talk fast. I had to concentrate and allow the words to sink in, then a few seconds later I usually understood at least half. I also realized she had erased her Cretan accent and never once slipped into the Cretan dialect.

I asked how she had decided to become an interior decorator. Stamatina told me she came to Athens for secretarial school, and afterward found a job with a decorator. He became her mentor, then five years later she started her own company. Stamatina mentioned some of her clients, and I recognized the names from politics and show business.

She's nice, I thought, watching her arrange white-chocolate cookies on an exquisite bronze tray. And artistic. I would have to scold Dimitris for keeping us apart so long.

Our coffee and conversation went well. I didn't always understand Stamatina, but Aristotelis paused frequently and phrased his sentences carefully. He was charming too, full of anecdotes about his work, again with names I knew from newspapers and television. Most of all, I appreciated that he didn't treat us like the hick village relatives we so obviously were.

We sat for over an hour. Everyone had refills on coffee, then Dimitris stood and said he couldn't recall where the toilet was.

"In the hall, next to the kitchen," Stamatina said. "And Dimitris? Would you please pee sitting down so you don't wet the seat or rug?"

One by one, the words sunk in. Had I heard correctly? Dimitris glared at her and stalked off. I looked at Stamatina and saw her worried gaze following Dimitris as he left the room.

I turned to Aristotelis. He had a gleam in his eye for me, a plea for understanding.

"So," he said, resuming our conversation, "how does it feel to be pregnant?"

"Great," I replied. "Although the truth is, I have moments when I feel scared about being a mother."

I thought we could go on talking and just forget Stamatina's comment. But then she jumped up from her seat, wringing her hands in anguish. She ran to the bathroom and knocked urgently on the door. "Dimitris? Did you do as I asked?"

Aristotelis sighed. "I would love to have children," he said in a low voice. "But we can't. Not with Stamatina the way she is."

Then I understood. Stamatina wasn't a good housekeeper, she was a unrelenting perfectionist. No wonder she excelled at her job: she created pristine environments and walked away before life intervened. I remembered reading once that there were three types of obsessive-compulsives: counters, checkers, and cleaners. Clearly Stamatina was a cleaner.

Dimitris emerged from the bathroom in a barely contained rage, and we left shortly after. We wouldn't be going back there any time soon. Then Dimitris—calm, reasonable Dimitris—stalked through the streets of Glyfada so quickly I could hardly keep up.

Finally I grabbed his wrist. "Slow down! Have you forgotten I'm pregnant?"

Dimitris stopped. He took me in his arms and told me he was sorry. We sat on the hood of a parked car to catch our breath.

"Now you know why I didn't want to go there," he said.

"Why didn't you tell me about this before?"

"You wouldn't have believed me."

Which was probably true. "Is that why Stamatina never comes to the village?"

"She can't bear the mess. Life is agony for her, you know."

"How does Aristotelis stay with her?"

Dimitris shrugged. "He loves her. And Stamatina loves him, as much as she can."

As much as she was able to love anyone with bodily functions, I thought. "Dimitris, why are you so normal when your sisters have so many problems?"

"Because I was raised by my aunt, not my father."

I never saw Stamatina again, although I kept in contact. I sent her and Aristotelis pictures of Aspasia, and I always called them on their name days and other holidays.

Back in the village after our visit, I mentioned Stamatina to Sophia just to see what she would say.

"Lots of money," Sophia told me. "Stamatina married well. But she's a *periptosi.*"

I didn't know what that meant. Back home, I looked up the word in my *Oxford Greek-English Learner's Dictionary*. That's when I learned that "She's a *periptosi*" meant "She's a nutcase."

I headed toward my father-in-law's house. Clutching the box with the howling kitten, I stayed in the shadows so no one from the *kafenia* could see me.

The kitten was tiny, I rationalized. She wouldn't take up much space. I would just make sure she ate decent meals for a few months until she was able to survive on her own. It was true we already had five cats, but two of them were males who lived mostly in the mountains. Then there was Spike, an overweight white cat who even at three years old showed no interest in sex or hunting.

Between Dagmar and shopping and the kitten, I was late to pick up Aspasia. Christos was one of the few Greeks I knew who cared about punctuality, at least in the evenings when he pawed the floor if he wasn't at the *kafenio* by seven. He couldn't live without his evening round of *prefa*, a distant cousin of bridge that required three players and knowledge of the convoluted scoring system. Christos was one of the best players in the village, a fact he was always eager to prove.

I hurried past homes lit and warm, others dark and mute, weaving in and out of the streets until I reached my father-in-law's house. Through a window covered by an intricate lace curtain, I could see light and little pieces of the living room.

Looking down at the box in my arms, I hesitated. I didn't want Christos to see the kitten because I couldn't bear to hear any sarcastic comments. A piece of plywood was resting against the front wall, so I placed it on top of the box and tucked the box in a dark corner of the concrete patio. I couldn't wait to see Aspasia's face when I told her about our new cat.

I knocked. There was a loud grunt from inside, then Christos opened the door. He was a tall, heavyset man with thick white hair, cold green eyes, and a deeply creased face. As he loomed in the doorway and looked down at me, his expression was twisted into its habitual scowl.

"*Kalispera*," I sang out. "Sorry I'm late, I had to—"

"Never mind. Take the child, they're waiting for me at the *kafenio*."

He stepped aside, and there she was, my daughter. Aspasia could have been my twin: same hazel eyes and dark blonde hair, same oval-shaped face, same even eyebrows and straight nose. "What did I need you for?" I sometimes teased Dimitris. "You didn't contribute anything at all."

I knew at once that something was wrong. I could tell by the distracted way Aspasia stared at the television, the tilt of her head as it rested against the back of the couch. She didn't jump up and throw herself at me when I walked into the room, in fact she barely glanced at me. She's sick, I thought. It must be the flu that's going around.

"Aspasia!" I called out cheerfully. "Mommy's here, let's go."

I picked up her coat and knapsack, watching as she rose listlessly. I turned to Christos. "Doesn't she feel well?"

"No. Wouldn't eat a thing, so I got angry with her."

My cheeks grew hot. "You don't get mad at a child for not eating, Christos." I refused to call him *baba*, although I had called my mother-in-law *mama* from the start. "Giving her dinner was your idea, but if you're going to get angry, then—"

"Enough!" he interrupted. "I didn't yell at her. Just the child should eat."

"Hmpf."

Christos and I had different ideas about child-rearing, and I had to watch him like a hawk. But although he had hit Dimitris and Pepina, I was absolutely certain he would never touch Aspasia.

Despite his disappointment that Aspasia was female and wouldn't carry his full name, Christos adored her. He came to see Aspasia every day when she was an infant, and later he enjoyed parading her around the village in a stroller. I knew this was showboating; he liked the image of big gruff Christos Theodorakis caring for his baby granddaughter. But Aspasia adored him, so I didn't mind.

Now that she was older, Christos liked to take Aspasia on his donkey when he went to inspect his olive trees and vineyards. Other times they went to the *kafenio*, where she sat on his knee and drank an orange soda while he played *prefa*. Aunt Hara scolded me about this, but I didn't see the harm—it wasn't as if he was taking her to a casino. I felt lucky that Christos was so willing to babysit, and I was the envy of all the young mothers in the village.

No one had a father-in-law as helpful as mine.

As Christos shut off the lights throughout the house, I knelt down in front of Aspasia and put a hand on her forehead.

"You don't feel well?" I asked in English.

She shook her head no.

"Where? Your tummy?"

A slow nod yes.

"Do you think you've got the same thing Despina had last week when she threw up at school?"

A shrug.

"I bet you do. When we get home, you can get into your pajamas and snuggle up on the couch under some blankets. I'll make us tea."

"OK," Aspasia whispered.

She was so solemn I had to swallow a smile.

"And guess what?" I said. "I've got a surprise, a really good one, but we need to leave before your *papoos* finds out." I stood and took her hand. "We're leaving, Christos," I called out.

"*Sto kalo*," he barked from the kitchen. Which meant "Go to the good."

Once outside, I led Aspasia to the corner of the patio. After taking off the piece of plywood, I lifted the box.

Aspasia clutched my coat sleeve. "Mommy, what's in there?"

"It's the gray kitten who lives by the store, the one we always feel sorry for. She's coming home with us."

I expected pleas to put down the box so Aspasia could see the kitten, but she stayed quiet. She must really be sick if a new kitten didn't perk her up.

As we walked home, I shifted the box under one arm and took Aspasia's hand. She held my fingers tightly as we made our way through the quiet village. I talked about English class and the pictures everyone had drawn, then told her how I caught the kitten. I didn't mention Old Manolies—I simply said I found the kitten in front of the store and managed to coax her into the box.

Eventually I fell silent. Accompanied by the occasional sound of the mewing kitten, we moved carefully on the cobblestone streets, mindful of the darkness pressing in on us.

As I turned onto our street, I noticed that Mrs. D had finally gone inside. Passing the house, I caught a glimpse of her on the couch, still wrapped in her nest of black shawls and watching a game show.

I opened the gate and stepped onto our concrete patio. I pushed open our door—we never locked it—and turned on the lights.

A typical village house has many small rooms, each with its own door to the outside. When we bought our house, it was the same, but Dimitris knocked down the walls and added a fireplace, creating an American-style living room. A short staircase to the left of the fireplace led to our bedroom, and another to the right went up to Aspasia's. The kitchen and bathroom remained at the front of the house.

Two of our cats darted inside as we entered. I shooed them out, then set the cardboard box on its side and opened the flaps. The kitten streaked across the room in a gray flash and went under the couch. Hopefully she would emerge in a day or two.

"All right, Ms. Aspasia, let's get you settled." I helped take off her coat and felt her forehead again. Nothing. "Go change into pajamas, and I'll put on water for tea. You want Mommy to come with you?"

She shook her head no. I kissed her cheek and went into the kitchen to put a pan of water on the stove. I filled a saucer with milk and tucked it under the couch, catching a flash of the kitten's terrified eyes. Afterward I went up to my bedroom for blankets and a pillow, bringing them downstairs and making up the couch for Aspasia.

I looked at the clock. Quarter past seven, only thirty minutes until *Lampsi*.

Back in the kitchen, I arranged crackers and cheese on a tray, and filled an infuser with herbs Aunt Hara had collected in the mountains. I dropped the infuser into the rolling water and poked my head into the living room. Aspasia was slipping under the blankets, clutching her pink bunny Tommy.

After pouring the tea into mugs, I carried the tray into the living room. I sat in a chair next to the couch, making small talk as I stirred honey into the tea.

"If you don't feel better tomorrow, you don't have to go to school. But your class is making butterflies, right? If you want to stay home, I can run over and get the supplies, or ask your teacher to save some for you. He did that before, remember, when you were going to make macaroni art, and you had a high fever. Do you want some tea?"

I filled a spoon and blew on it to cool down the water. Aspasia opened her mouth passively and let me trickle the tea onto her tongue.

Her illness made me restless. Usually in the evenings, Aspasia came into the kitchen and chattered while I cooked. After dinner we lay on the floor to color, or sat on the couch reading our English-language encyclopedia. At quarter to eight, we stopped to watch *Lampsi*, often with the volume low so we could continue coloring or reading.

Our routine was the same when Dimitris was home, except he did all the cooking, and sometimes during *Lampsi* he took Aspasia into her room so I could have a moment to myself. After *Lampsi* it was bath time, a story, then sleep.

Now with Aspasia sick and apathetic, I felt out of sync, almost like a child myself as I silently willed her to hurry up and get well.

"How's your stomach?" I asked.

She shrugged.

"You want to try eating a cracker? Just one?"

She shook her head no.

"That's all right," I said. "Maybe tonight we'll skip your bath. Do you want to go to bed now?"

"No!" Aspasia spoke up for the first time. "I want to stay with you, Mommy."

"Let's turn on the TV and watch *Wheel of Fortune*."

Which of course wasn't called that, but rather *O Trohos tis tihis*. The show humbled me whenever I considered myself fluent in Greek. Occasionally I guessed an answer, but usually when the Greek letters were scattered on the board, all I saw was alphabet soup. I understood the words once they appeared, but it was a matter of cultural fluency, of knowing a country's in-jokes.

Even after seven years in Greece, I still had so much to learn.

I sipped my tea and watched as the game show ended. After a string of commercials, the screen went black. Dramatic piano music boomed, and the word *Lampsi* filled the screen.

Translations of *Lampsi* varied. An English-language magazine that covered Greek news called it "The Shine," but to me "The Warm Glow" was a better fit. I didn't know why I liked the show so much, but I wasn't alone. If a television was on at 7:45 p.m. in Greece, the person was most likely watching *Lampsi*.

My addiction began several years earlier when I started watching to improve my Greek. Tuning into a soap opera helped train my ear, and since I read the plot descriptions in a weekly television guide, I usually knew what was going on. In time my listening skills improved, but by then it was too late: I was hooked.

The main storyline concerned Alexis Drakos' forbidden love for his stepmother, Virna. She loved him too, but she was too honorable to divorce Alexis' father, a ruthless businessman and compulsive cheater. The plot was a bit over-the-top, but the woman who played Virna was a fine actress who performed in classical theater in Athens. Most importantly, she was from Crete, so she was one of us.

Aspasia never seemed to listen or care when I watched *Lampsi*, but once she looked up from her book and asked why it was bad for Alexis to love his mother. I explained that Virna was his stepmother, so it wasn't wrong exactly, just odd.

"Why?" Aspasia asked. "He just loves her."

I considered saying that Alexis loved Virna like how a daddy loved a mommy, and it was wrong because Virna had raised Alexis since he was fifteen. This seemed like too much information, so instead I said Virna loved Alexis but was afraid of hurting her husband. Like when Aspasia had plans to play with Maria, but didn't want to make Despina feel bad.

Aspasia gave me a long, level look. Which meant my explanation hadn't satisfied her, and I could expect more questions soon.

She was difficult to fool, my daughter. Only a month before, Aspasia had raced into the kitchen and asked, "Mommy, where do people come from?"

I had already explained sex to her at least a dozen times, but I stopped what I was doing and once again started describing how the sperm meets the egg.

Aspasia waved a hand. "I know all that," she said. "I mean, where do people come from? How did people come to the earth?"

I looked at her. How indeed?

Later that evening, I took out the encyclopedia and showed Aspasia the drawing of humankind's ascent from ape to Homo sapiens. As best I could, I explained Charles Darwin's theory of evolution.

Aspasia listened carefully. When I was done, she said, "I don't agree. I think we came from spaceships."

So much for Darwin. I asked myself then, as I had many times before, where exactly had Aspasia come from? She was too much herself for me to presume I was the one who created her.

On tonight's episode of *Lampsi*, Alexis was marrying Lily, a reformed prostitute and his brother's ex-girlfriend. Virna was battling her conflicting emotions: she loved Alexis, but it was time to let him go.

Scenes of the traditional Greek ceremony—kissing the Bible, sharing wine, and wearing wreaths—were interwoven with images of Virna on the beach, and flashbacks of her and Alexis making love. I glanced at Aspasia to see how she reacted to the spicier bits, but her expression remained indifferent.

The final frame froze on Virna's tormented face, then the credits began to roll.

"Wow," I commented. "He really married Lily. Do you still want to skip your bath?"

Aspasia nodded.

"How about I read you a story down here, then I'll take you up to bed. Anything special you want to hear?"

She shook her head no.

I kissed Aspasia's forehead and went upstairs to her room. Beside the bed was a small bookcase with a pile of her favorite books on top. Not Dr. Seuss, that was too lively. *Caps for Sale*? We always read that.

Finally I decided on *Bread and Jam for Frances*, one of my favorites. I also picked up a Greek book in case Aspasia was too tired to listen to English. She understood and spoke English well, but she wasn't fully bilingual; Greek would always be her first language.

On the way out of the room, my glance fell on Aspasia's clothes, crumpled in a pile on the floor. I picked up her dress, tights, and underpants so I could put them in the hamper.

To my surprise, I felt something wet. I separated the clothes and saw that Aspasia's underpants were soaked through in the crotch.

Strange. Did Aspasia pee in her pants? That wasn't like her. She occasionally wet the bed when she was younger, but the last time was over a year ago.

I laid her underpants on top of the bureau and smoothed them out with my hand. They were her favorite pair, white with small pink hearts.

It took me a moment before I realized that Aspasia's underpants weren't wet with urine, but with a thicker substance. Milky with a faintly bitter smell.

Semen.

But how—?

I was so stunned I almost laughed. How could Aspasia have semen in her underpants? It was unthinkable.

Did her clothes somehow touch dirty sheets? No, that was impossible; Dimitris had been gone for months. Maybe at her *papoos*' house? Christos was over seventy, he probably didn't even get erections anymore.

Was it maybe glue, from some misguided childhood experiment? Like the odd things I used to do as a child, filling my belly button with shaving cream or rolling deodorant on my face.

Had Aspasia cut herself? There wasn't any blood. Maybe she told Christos she had an itch between her legs, and he gave her a tube of first-aid cream. Since Aspasia was only five, she had used way too much.

I sighed with relief. Yes, that must be the explanation.

Still, I needed to ask what happened. If something was bothering her, I wanted to know.

I left the underpants on top of the bureau and went down to the living room. After setting the books on the coffee table, I pulled my stool up to the couch and took Aspasia's hand. She wasn't hot, but her gaze was vacant.

"Honey," I said slowly. "Before we read the books, I want to ask you a question. Did something happen at your *papoos* today?"

Her eyes darted to mine, then moved away. In other words, yes.

I moved my stool closer and ran my hand up and down her arm. "Do you want to tell me about it?"

She shook her head no.

"Why not? Do you think I'll get mad?"

Aspasia thought for a moment, then shook her head again.

"So why don't you tell me?" I coaxed.

"I can't," she replied mournfully.

"Why?"

"Because my *papoos* said I couldn't."

A twist of anger shot through my chest. "Did he hit you?"

"No."

"You're telling the truth?"

"He didn't hit me, Mommy, I swear."

Time for another tactic. "Aspasia, I know your *papoos* said not to tell, but that doesn't mean you can't. It's like—remember your daddy's birthday last summer? The plate with the cake wouldn't fit in the refrigerator, so I had to pick up the cake with my hands and put it on a smaller plate."

"I remember," she said quietly.

"And remember I told you not to tell? But the next day we told your daddy anyway, and we all laughed? What I mean is—" What did I mean? "Sometimes 'Don't tell' isn't the same thing as 'Don't tell forever.'"

Aspasia looked confused, then burst out, "My *papoos* said if I told anyone, I'd have to live by myself in the woods like Aunt Eleni, and everyone would call me crazy and no one would be my friend. He said I'd have no food and I'd have to eat rats, but how maybe I'd die anyway from all the monsters."

Tomorrow, I told myself, I am going to find that man and give him the tongue-lashing of his life. How dare Christos frighten Aspasia to cover up his own carelessness! And by the way, there went the illusion that Aspasia didn't know about Eleni's problems.

"Mommy, *papoos* said something else too."

"What?"

"He said that if I told, someone would come and poison our cats."

This was unfortunately a favorite pastime for certain people in the village. It was supposedly a way to keep the feral-cat population under control, but I thought it was pure sadism.

Aspasia loved her cats as much as she loved Dimitris and me, so this was a particularly cruel thing for Christos to say. Anger burned up my throat.

"Aspasia, look at me. What your *papoos* said was completely untrue. Your daddy and I love you more than anything in the world, and we would never let anyone take you away from us. And we wouldn't allow someone to hurt our cats. Your *papoos* was very wrong to say what he did."

A spark of hope. "You won't send me away?"

"Nope."

"I won't have to live in the woods?"

"Never."

"And our cats will be OK?"

"Absolutely," I assured her. "Your *papoos* made up those stories to scare you. So tell me, what happened?"

Aspasia switched to Greek.

"I was in the living room coloring and my *papoos* was in the bedroom. He called for me to come, so I went in. He was lying on the bed and he told me to sit next to him. I did because I thought maybe he wanted to tell me a story. Then he asked if I wanted to see something and I said yes, so he pulled down his pants and he took out his thing."

I'm not hearing this, I thought. Aspasia had an itch. She told her grandfather, and he took her to the bathroom and handed her a tube of first-aid cream.

"*Papoos* asked if I'd ever seen one before, and I said I'd seen daddy's when we went swimming. He asked me if I knew it could do tricks. He said if I touched his thing, it would get big, and if I touched it a lot, water would come out. I told him I didn't want to touch it, b-but he took my hand and made me touch it and it got big."

You can't leave a five-year-old unattended with a tube of cream. What if Aspasia had swallowed some? Christos really wasn't an intelligent man.

"Then he picked me up and put me on top of his thing. I started to cry and he told me to stop crying. He kept pushing the thing against me, he pushed really hard and it hurt really bad. I cried more and told him to stop, but he didn't.

"Finally he did stop, and he told me I couldn't tell anyone because everyone would say I was crazy. I'd have to live alone in the woods with monsters, and all my cats would die. But now I don't believe him because you said he was lying."

Aspasia looked at me, her little tearstained face lifted hopefully.

"So I don't have to go live in the woods? And no one will hurt our cats?"

One morning during my pregnancy, Dimitris and I were lying in bed. He had his hand under my nightgown and was stroking my rounded belly.

"If it's a girl," he announced, "I want to name her Aspasia."

I laughed. "That's an interesting name! Why?"

He explained that the real Aspasia lived during the Golden Age of Greece. She was lover and advisor to Pericles and had founded her own school of rhetoric. Her best-known student was none other than Socrates, and in one of Plato's dialogues, Socrates praised Aspasia for her intelligence.

Dimitris said that when he read about Aspasia in school, he thought: When I have a daughter, I will name her Aspasia.

"OK," I said slowly. "If she was Socrates' teacher, that's pretty impressive. But isn't that too much for a little girl, to carry the name of someone so famous?"

He shook his head. "Here in Greece, we're proud of our heritage. If you give a child the name of a great person, they want to live up to that. Aspasia was perhaps the greatest Greek woman who ever lived, other than Melina Mercouri."

I smiled. "I guess we don't really have a choice. Aspasia it is. If the baby's a girl."

"Don't worry," Dimitris replied. "She will be."

I didn't want to believe her. But I had to. Aspasia was my child, and she had been hurt.

Raped.

But no, I didn't want to believe her! Because if her story were true—

As a child, I had lived in a perpetual state of fear. As an adult, however, I had only been truly afraid a few times: awaiting a laboratory report on an ovarian cyst, getting a phone call about an accident at Dimitris' jobsite, and once during a twisty ride in the Cretan mountains when I realized our bus driver was extremely drunk.

And now this.

My left hand began to flap uncontrollably. I wanted to run from the room, I wanted to cover my ears and scream, I wanted to grab Aspasia and catch a plane to anywhere. Here was my daughter lying on the couch, her hazel eyes—my eyes—begging me not to send her away to a forest full of monsters and crazy aunts, imploring me to protect her cats. I had to jump in and save the day, and I didn't know how.

A dozen questions formed on my lips, only to die there.

Are you sure—?

Maybe your *papoos* meant something else when he—?

And, worst of all, where was I at that moment? Why had I left my daughter alone with a man who hurt her?

From the moment Aspasia was born, I was afraid I would do something wrong and damage her. Dimitris couldn't understand my fear, no matter how hard I tried to explain. He used to tease me about it, but he stopped when he realized I was serious.

As Aspasia grew, I found myself growing too. I realized I was a competent, patient mother, and gradually the fear faded away.

And now, boom, it was back.

My mouth opened, but I didn't make a sound. How was I supposed to handle this? If I did nothing, would the moment go away?

But no, the moment stretched out, mute and unbearable, and my panic rose. I didn't want to ruin Aspasia for life.

Then, thank God, a million volts of anger exploded in my chest and shattered the panic. I was worried that *I* might ruin her? Her *papoos* hadn't been worried! All the responsibility, all the guilt, lay with him.

I was on Aspasia's side, and I always would be.

I moved from my stool to the couch and pulled Aspasia onto my lap. She put her arms around my neck and started to cry.

"It's OK," I said soothingly as I rocked her, my tears melting into her hair. "I'm here now, and everything's going to be all right."

I let her cry, trying to clear a space in my mind for thinking, for logic. Dimitris! I called to him inside my head, just as I did before I moved to Crete, when I was in America and he was so far away. I needed him here, but it was impossible. His ship had left Japan the previous day, and he wouldn't be docking at San Diego for at least another three weeks.

If I called the ship's main office in Athens, they could send Dimitris a message. But what would I write? YOUR FATHER RAPED ASPASIA. WHAT SHOULD I DO? The pain and helplessness would drive Dimitris mad. Better to wait until he docked at San Diego. Dimitris promised to fly back in case of an emergency, and this was an emergency.

The thought of my husband coming home calmed me a little, but then I realized it would be three weeks at least, more if they hit bad weather. That was a long time. Meanwhile, I had to keep Christos away from Aspasia.

As soon as I put her to bed, I would go over to Christos' house and rip his head off. But no, Aspasia needed me. What if she woke up in the middle of the night and found herself alone? I would wait until morning.

And maybe I shouldn't see Christos on my own. Perhaps I should go with Aunt Hara. Or even better, the police.

"Mommy?" Aspasia pulled her face away from my neck and looked up at me. Her eyelids were swollen and she needed a tissue.

"What, sweetie?"

"Can I have some water?"

"Sure."

I went to the kitchen and came back with a full glass and some napkins. I stroked Aspasia's hair as she drank in short, harsh gulps.

When she finished, I took her onto my lap, this time facing me. I held the napkins to her nose and told her to blow, then I wiped the tears from her cheeks, neck, and collarbone.

Now we were ready.

I swallowed painfully.

Voice shaking, I said, "Aspasia, I want to talk to you about what happened today. I need you to know that what your *papoos* did was very, very wrong. But you knew that, didn't you? That's why you said no and cried, right?"

Aspasia nodded.

"You were extremely brave to do all that. I'm really proud of you. And I want you to know that your *papoos* will never, ever do that to you again. I'll make sure of it."

"But Mommy, I go there every day."

"Not anymore."

Aspasia started crying again. I understood why: life without her *papoos* was unthinkable. Christos was an integral part of her daily routine, and although he had done this terrible thing, the good memories were stronger.

I rubbed her back. "I know you like going there, honey. But I can't leave you alone with your *papoos* anymore. We can't take the chance that he might do this again."

"But Mommy, I don't think he will! He knows I didn't like it, and if you tell him not to do it, he won't. Where will I go if I don't go there?"

"There's plenty of other places to go. First of all, you don't have to go anywhere. You could stay in your room and play while I teach. And if you promise not to be bossy, it's fine to join Despina and the others when they have class. There's also Aunt Hara's house, or maybe go play with Despina or Maria when they're free."

"I guess so," she said doubtfully.

"How do you feel now? How's your stomach?"

"It wasn't ever my stomach that hurt. It was my *lower* stomach."

My hand started to jump again. "Do you want me to look at your lower stomach?"

Aspasia wrinkled her nose. "No."

"You're sure?"

"I'm sure, Mommy."

I wanted to insist, but she had already been exposed enough in one day. And in truth, I wasn't strong enough to bear the sight of her.

"OK," I said. "Listen, do you want to sleep with me tonight?"

She nodded eagerly.

"All right. Brush your teeth and wash your face, then we'll go to bed."

As Aspasia walked slowly toward the bathroom, I fought an urge to follow her. Let her go, I told myself. She's not a cripple.

Numbly, I gathered the food and drinks onto the tray and carried everything into the kitchen. I took the bedding upstairs to my room and went into Aspasia's room to put the books back.

Her underpants were still on the bureau. I picked them up by the waistband and ran downstairs to the kitchen, where I stuffed them into the very bottom of the garbage can.

When Aspasia came out of the bathroom, I scooped her and Tommy into my arms and walked up the steps to my bedroom. It was a small room right up against the mountainside, warm and cozy.

Once under the covers, Aspasia clung to me and wept. I ran my hand up and down her back, her every sob just killing me.

I was almost asleep when a thought jolted me awake.

Why hadn't Christos cleaned up the semen?

I knew that if I'd done something so wrong—if I had committed a crime—I would do everything in my power to cover my tracks. Scaring Aspasia was one thing, but he hadn't even bothered to destroy the evidence.

Wasn't Christos worried I would see her underpants? Didn't he want to avoid getting caught? It was as if he felt invincible.

If Christos truly wasn't concerned, if he really felt that invulnerable, it signified an arrogance so huge it took my breath away.

My eyes grew heavy. I wanted to stay awake and think things through, but sleep was stronger than I was. Gradually my thoughts faded, and everything turned black.

Wednesday

I opened my eyes slowly.

It was morning. The clock read ten minutes to seven, so I had a little time before I needed to wake Aspasia. She was sleeping half on top of me, one warm, thin leg hooked around my knee.

I was still alive. Every breath hurt and I was sore all over. But it was morning, so I needed to get up. I had to think and I had to act.

My plan to rush out and confront Christos was impossible. I would be busy getting Aspasia ready for school until eight. By that time, Christos would be settled in the *kafenio*, in his chair at his table, drinking coffee and making sarcastic comments while waiting for someone to start a game of *prefa*.

I could pull Christos out of the *kafenio*, but I didn't want to make a public scene. Not because I wanted to protect him; it was Aspasia I needed to shield. This was her most personal business, and I didn't have the right to bring the whole village in on it. Not yet, anyhow.

Instead I would see Eleni, then have a cup of coffee with Aunt Hara as usual. Maybe I would tell her everything. Or maybe not. But after coffee, I would go find Christos at the *kafenio* and march him back to his house. Aspasia would be in school until noon, giving me time to make it clear he was never to go near my child again.

What about the police? Should I call and ask them to meet me at Christos' house? Maybe I would just bring Aunt Hara to see Christos, then when Dimitris came home, we could go to the police together. But even without involving the authorities, I could forbid Christos to see Aspasia.

Just the thought of him made me ill. A swirl of crackling red light slid before my eyes. The thing he had done to my daughter! The sick, horrible thing! I could scream for hours, and it still wouldn't dissolve an iota of my white-hot rage.

Seven o'clock. I ran my fingers through Aspasia's hair and softly said her name.

As I gently untangled her limbs from mine, Aspasia blinked, then opened her eyes wide. It was never hard to wake her.

"Hi, Mommy."

"Good morning, honey." I passed a hand over her forehead. She was warm, but she didn't have a fever. "How are you feeling? Do you think you can go to school?"

She nodded. "I want to make a butterfly."

"Good."

I hesitated. Should we talk about what happened? Did I need to tell Aspasia my plan to confront her *papoos*? I didn't want to force her to speak about everything again, but it wouldn't be right to pretend nothing had changed.

My goal had always been to spare Aspasia from the kind of surreal moments I had grown up with. Like when my favorite cat died, and my stepfather scornfully asked why I was crying. Incidents like that had left me confused for years, and I would not subject Aspasia to the same bewilderment.

Before I could decide what to do, Aspasia was out of bed and on the way to her room. I trailed after, watching her undress and choose her clothes, maroon wool pants and a smock with yellow, white, and maroon flowers. The top wasn't warm enough for winter, so she wore it over pink long underwear.

We went downstairs. Aspasia used the bathroom, then sat at the table in the corner of the living room, which was where we ate our meals. I cooked oatmeal and put two steaming bowls on the table, topping the oatmeal with raisins arranged in a smiley face.

Even though I wasn't the least bit hungry, I forced myself to eat. Aspasia carefully scooped up oatmeal around the raisin face, leaving the eyes, nose, and crooked mouth teetering on small oatmeal mountains.

I looked out the window. The sky was light gray with a dull sun—rain was on the way.

As I looked down at my bowl again, a fist of pain hit my belly. Dimitris! I cried out in my head. Oh, Dimitris. Because I couldn't go through this alone. I just couldn't.

While Aspasia continued to undermine the raisin face, I took one last bite of oatmeal and put my bowl in the sink. I went up to my room to change, then came downstairs to use the bathroom. Life goes on, I told my reflection as I brushed my hair in sharp pulls. Life goes on.

Aspasia joined me in the bathroom and brushed her teeth, opening her mouth wide afterward so I could inspect her handiwork.

"Perfect," I declared. "Now let's get your knapsack ready."

"It's already ready. I didn't take anything out last night."

"Is it OK if I walk you to school?"

She thought for a moment. "I guess so."

This was a major victory. Aspasia never wanted me to go with her to school. If I had to accompany her for some reason, I was always banished five steps behind.

But even if Aspasia had said no, I still would have gone. She was no longer safe on her own, not with my predatory father-in-law roaming about. I had always been determined not to be a smothering mother, but after what had happened, I could understand the appeal of never letting your child out of your sight.

We put on our coats, and Aspasia grabbed her knapsack. A gift from one of my friends in America, it was pink and decorated with a smiling purple dinosaur. Aspasia was the only child in the village with such an exotic knapsack, and she rarely left the house without it.

I opened the front door, and we stepped onto the patio. Instantly we were greeted by Mrs. D, as always in black and sitting on her bench. *"Kalimera!"* she called.

"Good morning," I replied, trying to sound cheerful.

We crossed the patio, and I opened the gate. As I shut it behind me, Mrs. D said, "Not walking by yourself this morning, Aspasia? Maybe that's because your mommy has an errand to run."

Mrs. D looked at me significantly. Everyone knew about my trips to see Eleni. As for Aspasia, she stared at Mrs. D and furrowed her brow. She found Mrs. D as annoying as I did.

"Here." Mrs. D pushed a napkin-covered cookie into Aspasia's hand. "You can eat it on your break."

Aspasia looked up to see my reaction, but I just smiled. "Thank you," I said. "Although you know it's not good for her to eat too many sweets."

"One cookie won't hurt. Katerina, after you left with the children last night, Haralambis was here. I heard when he knocked, so I came out and told him you weren't home. Did he find you? I said you were probably at the *kafenio*."

"I didn't see him, no."

"That's a pity. I know Haralambis worries about you, being alone without your husband. You miss your daddy, don't you?" Mrs. D cackled at Aspasia, baring her naked gums. "How many months has he been away?"

"Four," I answered, my chest sore.

"That's not long at all. Why, my Mr. D was a sailor too, and I remember whenever he—"

"Mrs. D," I said firmly. "We have to go."

"Of course, don't let me stop you. *Sto kalo*."

Aspasia gave me the cookie to put in her knapsack, then she took my hand.

We were late, so we ran down the cobblestone street, flying past a row of houses and a tied-up donkey. Around another corner past the church, the school came into view, a low white building with a bare front yard. About twenty children were running toward the doorway, where three teachers stood smiling and clapping their hands.

Aspasia shot me a triumphant look: we made it! She released my hand and ran to join the others, wedging in beside Despina so they could enter together.

The last child went inside, the teachers waved at me and the other mothers, then the large wooden doors slammed shut.

She was gone.

As I walked to my car, I could sense Christos.

That peculiar crackling red light tumbled before my eyes. I knew that if I turned my head to the right, I would see his face through the *kafenio* window. My body pulsed with an anger so dizzying I was afraid I might faint.

"Katerina! Katerina!"

Aunt Hara was standing next to my car. I waved and quickened my pace.

A short, round woman with a pouty smile and a puff of brown hair, Aunt Hara never said her exact age, but I knew she was nearing sixty. As always, she was dressed all in black. Her husband had died two years before, so that was her color from now on.

"*Kalimera*," she greeted me when I reached the car. "Didn't you see? I was waving my arms."

"Sorry, I was distracted."

"I have something for Eleni." She pointed to several bulging plastic bags on the hood of the car. "I went to your house but you had already left, so I came here to wait for you."

"I walked Aspasia to school, that's why I wasn't home."

She nodded. "Mrs. D told me."

I examined the "something" that Aunt Hara had brought. Two hunks of cheese, homemade cookies, fresh mushrooms, two loaves of bread, a large pot of beans cooked in olive oil and tomato sauce.

"Do you think that's enough?" she asked worriedly.

"It's more than enough," I assured her.

I opened the trunk to put in the food. Aunt Hara leaned over to inspect my purchases, rummaging inside each bag.

"Good, Eleni needs spaghetti . . . Is that enough tampons? . . . Next time you should get four chocolate bars."

I watched Aunt Hara repack my groceries, then put in her own bags. "Drive slow," she warned me. "You don't want the beans to spill over. Oh, and this . . ."

Aunt Hara reached into the pocket of her sweater and pulled out a palm-sized icon of Saint Minas riding his white horse.

"A man came through the village selling them. I bought one for me and one for Eleni. And one for you too, I have it at home."

She looked at me wistfully, full of hope for my long-awaited—and never to be—conversion to Greek Orthodoxy. The Christianity in my childhood home had been smothering, and I had no intention of recreating it here.

"Thank you. I better go now."

"Give my love to Eleni. Come by after, Yaya and I will be waiting."

"OK."

As I reversed the car, I deliberately avoided looking at the *kafenio*. I drove out of the village center and turned left onto the main road.

After half a minute, I made a right onto a dirt road that ascended into the foothills of the mountains behind our village. Olive trees surrounded both sides of the car as far as I could see, some young and thin, others old and gnarled. Their silver-green leaves flashed in the dim November sun, and a few overhanging branches scraped the roof of the car.

I came to a fork in the road. One way went up into the mountains, the other went down into a gorge. I followed the latter, and now the olive trees I passed belonged to us.

The road descended until it hit a riverbed, wide enough to drive on, but quite rocky and not good for the car. The riverbanks steepened, and then I was in a gorge with rock faces looming over me. The riverbed twisted sharply, the walls of the gorge lowered, and up on the right side I could see Eleni's house.

My stomach tightened. I never liked coming here.

I parked and got out of the car. Eleni's dog started barking, but otherwise everything was deeply silent.

"*Ya soo*," a voice rang out from above me. "Do you need help?"

"Yes," I called back.

"I'm coming."

I went to the back of the car and opened the trunk. When I looked up, I saw Eleni picking her way down the steep path, followed by her hairy yellow dog, Platon.

Eleni was tall and thin with large brown eyes and shoulder-length brown hair that she always wore pulled back. In her black stretch pants and long red sweater, she looked like any woman spending the morning at home.

She smiled, but not exactly. We had several years of tension between us, and we both knew I had come against my will. But Eleni wasn't awkward; she never apologized or explained herself, and she never seemed embarrassed about being a grown woman who had to be shopped for. Instead I was always the one who was self-conscious, bumbling my words and laughing for no reason.

That morning was no exception. I made nervous conversation as I petted Platon, then loaded Eleni's arms with shopping bags.

"I bought you dishwashing liquid, Sophia said you needed it. Also garbage bags and matches. Aunt Hara made these beans for you, it's quite a lot and they might go bad since you don't have a refrigerator, but I guess you have your tricks for keeping things fresh."

Eleni didn't say a word. I picked up Aunt Hara's pot, then we climbed the steep path with Platon at our heels.

When we reached the top, I stopped to catch my breath. It was a lovely house, small and white with gray shutters and a cobblestone patio. A gnarled carob tree dominated the front yard, and tidy flower beds lined the edge of the house. Two black-and-white cats lay under the tree, curled around each other and fast asleep.

We went into the tidy little kitchen. A battery-powered radio stood on a table in the corner, rectangles of embroidered cloth hung on the walls, and a small window with a gray shutter was cracked open to let in the cool air.

I sat down at the wooden table and watched Eleni put everything away. When she was finished, she would as usual offer me tea, which I would as always drink so quickly that I burned my mouth.

Suddenly out of nowhere, the fist of pain in my stomach returned. Hot patches formed under my eyes, and I was a breath away from bursting into tears.

No! I told myself. Not here! I can't cry in front of Eleni.

The warmth under my eyes grew hotter. I put a finger on one and was shocked to feel its hard soreness. The pressure was intense, building steadily until the tears pushed up and raced down my face.

Eleni set the dishwashing liquid on the counter. "Why, Katerina!"

She sat across from me and took my hand. I laid my head on my arms and wept. The crackling red light started again, now joined by purple and blue and a horrible yellow. The yellow spread and pushed away the other colors and I was lost, drowning in a vile mustard cloud. From a distance I could hear my gasping and hiccupping, as well as faint murmurs from Eleni as she tried to comfort me.

Slowly I calmed down. The yellow faded into a pale peach, which eventually vanished into black.

I opened my eyes and raised my head, hugging my arms around my waist. My chest was tight and painful. It was as if someone had died.

That's when I understood that something had died. My beautiful daughter's innocence. It was gone, never to return.

It was hard to meet Eleni's gaze, but I had to. She was staring at me sympathetically, handing over a wad of napkins so I could blow my nose.

"I thought I was supposed to be the crazy one," she commented.

"You aren't—" Then I stopped. I didn't know what to say.

"Are you crying because you miss Dimitris?" Eleni asked. "Or has something particular happened?"

I couldn't tell her. We were not on good terms, and Christos was her father. So I lied, babbling something about the pressures of being a single mother, my English classes, keeping the house clean . . .

"And on top of that," Eleni said wryly, "you have to shop for your sister-in-law. Sophia can come here if it's too much for you."

I knew Dimitris would be disappointed if I asked Sophia to take care of a family matter. "No, I can manage."

"Do you want some tea?"

"Please."

Eleni lit the gas stove and put on water to boil. We sat silently as the water gained momentum, then my mouth opened and I found myself asking, "Do you ever want to get married again?"

"No," Eleni answered at once. "My husband was the only man I'll ever love." She paused. "But I get offers."

"You do?"

"Pretty often. Although not exactly for marriage."

"What do you mean?"

"I'm a woman living alone in the mountains. I'm also a woman who slept with over a dozen men in the village when she was a teenager. People here don't forget things like that. Especially the men." She brought out two teacups, put an infuser with herbs in each one, then turned off the gas and filled the cups with boiling water. "Would you like some chocolate?"

"Sure. But tell me, do the men come here? Do they speak to you?"

"They try," Eleni replied. She took a chocolate bar out of a drawer, then took off the wrapper and broke it into pieces. "The ones I've slept with, and the ones I haven't slept with. Most are married with children."

She reeled off a list names that stunned me. They were all men in our village who I saw every day. Most of them were in their thirties and forties, although some were even older.

"I had no idea," I said slowly. "Does Dimitris know?"

"He bought me a shotgun."

"What!? Dimitris never told me that."

"He didn't want to worry you."

"Where's the gun now?"

"In the bedroom, on top of the bookshelf. I've only had to fire it once. Usually it's enough if I take it out and wave it." Eleni raised an eyebrow. "Having the reputation as the village crazy is helpful at times."

I absorbed this new information in stunned silence. All those men! Could it be true?

But I felt sure that Eleni wasn't lying. Because the same thing had happened to me in high school. College, too. Back when I used to drink. Only one person in the village knew about the old me—Katherine—and that was Dimitris. Otherwise it was my secret to keep, day in and day out.

As we drank our tea, Eleni asked if I had heard from Dimitris, and I told her about his most recent letter. She said it was generous of him to make such a sacrifice for me, and I nodded numbly.

We fell silent. I played with my teaspoon, searching for something to say. Eleni stared down at the table and smoothed out the chocolate bar wrapper.

I swallowed the last of my tea in one greedy gulp. "It's getting late," I said, standing to leave. "I'm sorry I broke down in your kitchen."

Eleni shook her head. "Don't worry about that."

We walked outside. I gave Platon a final pat, then stood a moment to look at the house with its carob tree, flower beds, and peaceful animals.

"It's lovely here," I said slowly. "I always saw this place as, I don't know, some sort of punishment. But it's not, is it?"

"No," Eleni replied. "Not at all."

When I got to my car, I turned and looked up. I waved one more time, and Eleni waved back.

As I nosed the car onto the road leading out of the gorge, puzzle pieces that had been floating in my mind for years suddenly snapped into place. I realized something that had been staring me in the face ever since I moved here.

I stopped the car and slammed a palm against the steering wheel. But of course! How could I have been so blind?

Aunt Hara must know the truth. And if she didn't, I would find someone who did.

I restarted the car and drove quickly to the village.

As usual, I pushed open the door to Aunt Hara's living room without bothering to knock.

Aunt Hara and Yaya were sitting in their customary places on the couch. Aunt Hara was crocheting and Yaya was bent over the coffee table, carefully picking small stones from a heap of lentils on a white plate.

I said hello, then went outside again and passed through another door into the kitchen. I made myself coffee and carried it back into the living room, where I sat down in the armchair. The usual plate of sweets sat on the coffee table. I reached out and took a *ladokouloura*, a Cretan cookie made with olive oil, orange juice, and cinnamon.

It was a cozy, comfortable home. The furniture was the same as most homes in the village, heavy wooden couches and chairs with rough beige-and-brown floral fabric. The walls were crowded with souvenirs from Dimitris' travels—a purse from China, a mask from Africa, wooden dolls from Russia.

Tucked among the souvenirs were icons of saints from the Greek Orthodox canon, along with numerous versions of the *mati*, the blue-and-white charm used to ward off the evil eye. A *mati* even dangled from the handle of the wood-burning stove.

All the horizontal surfaces were crammed with framed pictures of family and friends. There were, however, no photos of children or grandchildren. Aunt Hara's husband had been sterile, a fact she shared with anyone who asked and even those who didn't. She handled her disappointment by filling the role of surrogate mother for those who needed her, myself included.

It took me a long time to understand Aunt Hara. When I first came to Crete, she was polite but chilly. Only when I became pregnant did she truly warm to me. Later, I asked her why she'd been so reserved, and she explained it was partly because I was foreign, and partly because she feared I would try to control Dimitris.

"You could if you wanted to," she said, "but I see that you don't and I'm glad."

Aunt Hara wasn't educated but she was shrewd, and over the years I'd come to trust her judgment. Her theory was that every marriage had a boss. She freely admitted that she'd been in charge in her own marriage.

"Unlike my poor sister Pepina," she added. "Such a mistake to marry that bully Christos."

As usual, we began our morning coffee by discussing *Lampsi*.

"We were just talking about Alexis and Lily," Aunt Hara said without looking up from her crocheting. "What do you think?"

"Big mistake," I replied, wiping cookie crumbs off my pants. "The marriage won't last six months, unless she gets pregnant."

"Poor Virna," Yaya said. "She'll never have any peace."

Yaya was Aunt Hara's mother, a tiny woman with a mustache, startling blue eyes, and long white hair in a braid. As always she was dressed in black, still officially in mourning for a husband she lost long ago, though she rarely mentioned him.

I loved Yaya, and I always enjoyed her company. Yaya's mind was still sharp and her memory prodigious, something she liked to prove by reciting the names of all the villages on our side of Crete. She didn't wear glasses despite her eighty-three years, and she was able to pick out minuscule stones from piles of lentils, something even I had trouble doing.

"They showed the commercial again last night," Yaya said to no one in particular.

"Don't start, *mama*," Aunt Hara warned. "I mean it, don't you dare."

The actress who played Virna was performing in a play in Athens, and Yaya's fondest desire was to go see her. Dimitris had promised to bring Yaya, but now of course he was at sea, and the only person who could take her was Aunt Hara.

"They still have tickets," Yaya went on. "We could get the boat tomorrow night and stay with your great-aunt."

"I'm not going to Athens," Aunt Hara declared. "I hate it there and you know it. Wait until next year, Dimitris will be back then."

Yaya sighed and shook her head. "Next year I'll be dead." She closed her eyes and rested her cheek on her palm, illustrating how she would look on her deathbed.

"So you keep promising," Aunt Hara snorted. "You've been saying that since you were sixty."

"I'm old and I'm going to die. Then you'll spend the rest of your life regretting that you didn't take me."

Aunt Hara rolled her eyes.

"And you know," Yaya went on, "if we're going to Athens, we might as well see Aliki. She's in a musical."

Aliki Vougiouklaki was the Brigitte Bardot of Greece, the "National Star" as the newspapers called her. Bringing up her name was particularly wicked of Yaya because when Aunt Hara was young, she could have been Aliki's twin. But although both women were near sixty, Aliki was still blonde and stunning, and she still had a waist, something Aunt Hara had lost years ago.

"Aliki!" she sniffed. "How many facelifts has that woman had? The back of her ears must be a fright."

"Why shouldn't she get her face lifted?" Yaya countered. "She looks beautiful."

"Melina never had a facelift."

Actress and international icon Melina Mercouri was sacred in this household. "You can't compare Aliki and Melina," Yaya said, crossing herself. "No one can live up to Melina, God bless her."

Aunt Hara sighed. "At least we agree on something."

Yaya looked at me and winked.

Aunt Hara pushed the plate of cookies toward me.

"Katerina, *ela*, take another. Tell us about Eleni, how is she? Does she have enough food?"

"Don't worry," I replied. "She has plenty. We even had a conversation today, believe it or not."

"Thank God!" Aunt Hara put down her crocheting, then took one of the icons off the wall and gave it a big kiss. "I've been praying for this moment. Does this mean you'll let Aspasia see her now?"

"Aunt Hara," I said sternly. "For years, you and Dimitris have told me that Eleni has mental problems. Then you both act like I'm a monster for not taking Aspasia to see her. I was just protecting my child. Surely you can understand that."

"We told you Eleni used to have problems. We never said she does now."

"Fine, but how am I supposed to believe that when I don't even know what's wrong with her? How can I be sure Eleni won't hurt Aspasia somehow?"

Aunt Hara snorted. "You're being ridiculous."

"Am I? Any time I ask about Eleni, I never get a straight answer. If you won't tell me what happened, I can only imagine the worst."

Yaya had stopped working. Her wide blue eyes darted between Aunt Hara and me.

Aunt Hara fussed with her crocheting, avoiding my gaze. Finally she looked up and said, "Eleni made up stories, that's all, crazy stories. It's true she tried to kill herself and stayed at a hospital, but that was a long time ago. I've told you before and I'll swear to it again, Eleni would never hurt a child." She paused. "So you'll bring Aspasia to see her?"

"N–not right now," I stammered. "Aspasia needs time. She'll be scared to go to Eleni's, she's heard stories from—from people."

"You mean Christos," Yaya snorted. "As if anyone can trust that man."

Guilt ripped through me.

"I'm going to make more coffee," Aunt Hara said, hoisting herself off the couch. "Katerina, do you want another? Not you, *mama*, your blood pressure is high enough as it is."

Aunt Hara left. She wasn't going to tell me the truth, so I sat up straight and stared at Yaya.

"I know," I whispered. "About Christos and Eleni."

It was a bluff, but it worked. Yaya closed her eyes and sighed. "So Eleni told you."

"She did."

Yaya nodded mournfully. "You're part of this family, you deserve to hear the truth."

"What's your version? Quick, before Aunt Hara comes back."

Yaya glanced at the door, then leaned forward and said swiftly, "When Eleni was twelve, she came here one day and said that Christos had been taking her to the mountains and making her have—you know, sex. She said he'd been doing it for years. Hara didn't believe her, and she said so."

I swallowed hard.

"Eleni never spoke to us about it again," Yaya went on. "When she got a little older, she started going around with boys. Then one day, she went into the *kafenio* when Christos was there, and she started screaming in front of everyone that he had sex with her. After that she ran home and slit her wrists."

"Oh my God." I was silent a moment. "Did you believe her?"

"Bah, no. Eleni was just making up stories to get attention. Christos is a bad man, but he'd never do anything like that."

"But Yaya, you don't know that for sure! Why would Eleni—"

The kitchen door slammed. Yaya put a finger to her lips and returned to the lentils.

Aunt Hara came in and set a cup of coffee in front of me. "I didn't tell you, Katerina, but Yaya and I watched *Kalimera zoe* last night. It's not as good as *Lampsi*, but I enjoyed it."

Yaya disagreed, of course. She hadn't liked the show, and she couldn't understand why Aunt Hara had wasted her time watching it.

The conversation carried on, but I didn't hear a word. I was thinking. And what I was thinking was that Christos hadn't cleaned up the semen because he was sure he wouldn't get caught. And the reason Christos was sure he wouldn't get caught was because he had done this before.

Christos had gotten away with it then, and he believed he would get away with it now.

I excused myself and ran outside. I vomited cookies, coffee, chocolate, tea, oatmeal, and raisins into a patch of flowers.

Aunt Hara ran after me, calling back to Yaya, "It must be the flu that's going around."

I hurried away from the house, assuring Aunt Hara and Yaya that I was heading home to rest.

But I couldn't bear to be shut up inside, so instead I went on a walk in the valley, my mind reeling from what Yaya had just told me. I walked and I thought and I cried, barely taking in the lush landscape of clover and olive trees.

At quarter to twelve, I went to pick up Aspasia. I was about to turn into the alley leading to the school when I froze. At the end of the alleyway, sitting on a wall in front of an abandoned stone house, I saw Christos. His back was to me, and he was facing the school.

Christos was waiting. For my daughter.

I ducked behind a house and watched him. Did Christos do this every day? I didn't think so. He was waiting because he was planning to talk to Aspasia, to see if she had told me what happened. Maybe Christos intended to reiterate his threats. Or worse, perhaps he was waiting simply because he wanted to see her.

The horrible truth rose up within me. Christos wasn't going to leave Aspasia alone. Something had started, and he would now seek—or even create—opportunities to be alone with her.

"Can the child come with me to the vineyards? You know she loves riding on the donkey."

"Go shopping in the city if you want, Katerina. I'll babysit this afternoon."

"If your friend wants you to visit her in Heraklion, go and stay the night. The child can sleep at my house."

Christos and Aspasia already had a unique bond, so no one would suspect a thing. Everyone in the village knew she was her *papoos'* pride and joy. Probably it had been the same with Eleni. I had even seen old photos of them riding on a donkey together, with Eleni about the same age as Aspasia.

Everyone had been oblivious to what was going on. But Christos' wife Pepina must have known. Surely Eleni had told her, since Eleni apparently told the entire village. I had no proof, but instinct told me Pepina had been aware all along.

And was it just Eleni? Probably Stamatina too.

Maybe Pepina had tried to confront Christos, but he beat her into silence. Or perhaps she was too terrified to say a word, and instead avoided her daughter's—daughters'—eyes when they came home after an afternoon in the mountains with their father.

I would never know. But there was one thing I knew for sure. I wasn't that kind of mother. My child had told me what had happened, and I believed her. More, I had promised to protect her.

A violent wave of nausea lurched through my stomach. Oh God, I thought, although I'm not the praying type. Please, make Christos leave her alone.

But God wouldn't help me, nor would all the icons in Aunt Hara's living room. No *mati* was big enough to repel a man like Christos. This was my battle, and I had to defend my child.

"But how?" I whispered. "How?"

I decided to begin by stopping Christos from ambushing Aspasia on her way home from school.

After backing out of the alley, I took an intricate route through the village streets, eventually emerging at the north end of the school. A few mothers stood in the yard chatting, I waved and called out hello.

Instead of joining the others, I sat on the low stone wall surrounding the school, where Christos couldn't see me. A cypress tree stood next to the wall, and I leaned against it for support while I stared at the school's wooden doors.

My situation was clear. No one would believe me, and no one would help me.

I could just hear Aunt Hara: "Aspasia's making up a story. She saw something on television, and that's how she got the idea."

But I saw her underpants! There was semen!

"Bah, you thought it was semen. You made a mistake."

But Aspasia told me it happened, and she never lies!

"Don't be silly, all children lie."

I always thought Aunt Hara was wonderful for taking in Dimitris and raising him as her own. But why didn't Aunt Hara help Eleni and Stamatina? How could she save one child and not the others? Yaya was no better; she had known everything, and she had done nothing.

As for the police, that was a joke. The station, located three villages away, had two men on the force. The captain was Christos' godson, and the other officer was the son of one of Christos' card-playing buddies. If I went to the station and told my story, they would try to talk me out of it, just as everyone had tried to talk Eleni out of her truth.

It wouldn't even matter that I had proof. I could take Aspasia's underpants out of the garbage, seal them in a plastic bag, and bring them to the police. The men would surely smirk when I handed over the bag and demanded they test it. I could also envision their phony regret when they later told me the evidence had mysteriously disappeared on its way to the police laboratory in Athens.

If I insisted they question Christos, the men would come to the village all rolling eyes and reluctance. They would find Christos at the *kafenio*, where they would apologize for taking him away from his card game and ask to speak in private.

Christos would deny everything. The officers would shrug and say, "We knew it wasn't true, but we had to do our job. What's wrong with your daughter-in-law anyway? Why is she spreading these stories about you?"

"Foreigners," Christos would retort. "You know how it is when foreign women try to live here. Either they leave after a few years, or they stay and go crazy."

Christos would slap the policemen on the back and invite them to the *kafenio* for a glass of *raki*, and the whole matter would be forgotten.

But not by Christos. He would start a whispering campaign against me. "I'm worried about Aspasia," he would say to the *kafenio* at large. "Katerina won't let me see her. But then Katerina has been acting strange lately, have you noticed?"

There were plenty of things Christos could criticize about me. Just by virtue of being foreign and having different habits, I was considered odd. Like that very moment. I was sitting all by myself and not gossiping with the other mothers.

Probably they thought nothing of it, since I rarely joined them. But with a steady push from Christos' side, they would soon be agreeing with him. "Katerina is so peculiar! We were at the school standing together and talking, and she was sitting off by herself. What's wrong with her?"

I had seen it happen to others, the slow and deliberate expulsion from village life. Shunning, the Amish called it, when a community punished one of their own with silence. Or another word, with origins in ancient Greek: ostracism.

Certainly I could start my own campaign against Christos. But it was doomed to fail because I was foreign. Not one of them, never was and never would be.

And because Christos was so devious, he would turn himself into the victim. That's what he did with Eleni. People often said, "Poor Christos, his own daughter won't speak to him" or "Such a pity, Eleni won't give Christos any grandchildren."

But never mind all that. I could handle the whispers, and I could put up with the shunning. I didn't give a damn. The point was, Christos would go unpunished. Which meant nothing would stop him from trying again, either with Aspasia or another child.

Dimitris! I called out to him in my head. If I could keep Aspasia from Christos for the next three weeks, Dimitris would take care of everything when he came back. He would believe Aspasia, and he wasn't afraid of his father or anyone else.

Just a few weeks, I told myself. As soon as Dimitris gets to San Diego, he can fly back to Greece and we can do this together. As a family.

A bell rang shrilly. The wooden doors burst open, and children streamed into the yard, a mass of colored coats and swinging knapsacks.

Standing up, I searched for Aspasia in the swarm of bodies. I looked toward the door and saw her coming out with her teacher beside her, his hand resting on her back.

I ran up to meet them, my heart pounding wildly. She hadn't told him, had she? No, Aspasia, don't tell anyone, not yet! I still needed time to figure out what I wanted to do.

They stopped when they saw me. Aspasia clutched a butterfly made of cardboard and gaily colored tissue paper. Her face was closed and her eyes dull. I knelt in front of her and took her hands, then looked up at the teacher.

"Aspasia doesn't feel well," he told me. "We made the butterflies and then she just sagged. There was only an hour left, so I didn't bother to call you." He patted her on the head. "It must be the flu that's going around."

"Probably," I agreed with a false smile.

"But Aspasia made a lovely butterfly, didn't you?" the teacher said.

"It certainly is beautiful." I took the butterfly gently out of her hand. "Does it have a name?"

"Bill," Aspasia said, pronouncing it "Beell."

"For the new president," I laughed. "Very good."

I thanked the teacher, then Aspasia and I walked out of the yard. She had made it through the morning on sheer willpower, but now she had nothing left.

In a few moments, we were going to run into Christos. Or maybe not. Perhaps he would go away if he saw that Aspasia wasn't alone. Maybe he would feel ashamed.

That hope turned out to be naive. As we passed by the church, I could see Christos sitting on the wall in front of the abandoned house. He saw us, and he stood up. But instead of leaving, Christos stayed right where he was.

I only had a brief moment before Aspasia noticed him.

"So," I said hastily, "today you'll stay with me. We'll eat lunch, you can have a nap, then Gogo is coming for her lesson at three. After that I have the fourth graders, then Spiros will be here. You can play in your room, or you can sit and listen if you're quiet. OK? You won't be going to *papoos'* house."

Aspasia nodded. "Do you think the kitten will come out?" she asked.

"Maybe. Remember how Spike was when we first got him? He stayed under the couch for two weeks."

Aspasia tightened her grip. She had seen Christos.

I looked up and forced myself to smile at him. He can't know that I know, I thought. Not until I decide what to do.

"What are you doing here?" Christos bellowed at me.

"Aspasia's stomach hurt, so I came to get her." I tried to sound breezy, but without much success.

"If the child is sick, why did you let her go to school?"

"She wanted to make a butterfly. But she's still not well," I said firmly, "so I'll keep her at home this afternoon."

"Don't be silly. The child can come to my house, she can lay down on the couch."

"*Ela*, Christos, I can't ask you to mind her when she's ill."

"Zucchinis!" Which was Greek for "ridiculous." "How can you teach if she's there? Give me the child, I'll take care of her."

He wasn't going to make this easy, was he?

"No need," I said, waving the suggestion away. "Aspasia will be fine with me. You know how it is when you're sick, you want to be in your own bed."

Christos pursed his lips. Was he looking at me suspiciously? That crackling red folded over my eyes, and I could no longer see him clearly.

"We'll be off now," I announced. "*Ya soo*."

"*Ya*." He bent over to kiss Aspasia, but I pulled her away before he had a chance.

We're safe, I thought, grabbing Aspasia's hand tighter as we hurried away. For the rest of the day, we're safe.

Thursday

The next morning when Aspasia and I came out of the house, Mrs. D was speechless. But not for long.

"You're walking Aspasia to school again? That's two days in a row! Is something wrong, is she afraid?"

I closed the patio gate behind us, and we stood in front of Mrs. D and her bench. The sky was the color of iron and the air was sullen; in a day or two, it would rain.

Breathing deeply, I jammed my fists into my coat pockets so they wouldn't fly out and knock Mrs. D off her seat. I wanted desperately to tell Mrs. D to fuck off, but I knew if I did, I would live to regret it.

Truth be told, I needed Mrs. D. Sometimes I asked her for a lemon or some flour instead of going all the way to the store. And occasionally Mrs. D watched Aspasia while I ran an errand or went to Aunt Hara's.

Mrs. D also needed me. I was the one who refilled her bottle of cooking gas and lugged it into her kitchen, and I drove her whenever she had a medical appointment. When Dimitris was home, he was at Mrs. D's house at least twice a week, helping out with some real or imagined task.

A village wasn't like a city where you hired strangers to help you. Our lives were deeply intertwined, and there were no strangers. So I didn't tell Mrs. D to fuck off. Instead I managed a smile and said, "Why don't you join us? The walk will do you good."

Aspasia looked at me and raised her eyebrows in horror.

Mrs. D waved a hand and cackled wildly. "Oh, you're a funny one! My goodness, I couldn't possibly. You two go along without me."

After we turned the corner, Aspasia took my hand. "Mommy, you didn't really want Mrs. D to come with us, did you?"

I squeezed her fingers lightly. "No, honey. I was just joking."

No sign of Christos on the way to school. I spent the morning at Aunt Hara's, then a half hour before school ended, I hid behind the church and waited to see if Christos would resume his post in front of the abandoned house. Thankfully he didn't come, and Aspasia and I managed to get home without seeing him.

At lunchtime, Aspasia stared down at her black-eyed peas without interest. "Mommy," she asked, "what are we going to do about *papoos* today?"

"Nothing," I said firmly. "You're staying here."

"Can I?"

"Of course. You'll be in your room when the sixth graders come, and you'll join Despina and the others later."

Aspasia looked relieved. Something had changed: she was no longer afraid of losing Christos, now she was just afraid. Instinctively Aspasia knew, as I did, that he was after her.

But we were so safe and whole in the warmth of our home that I wondered if perhaps I was exaggerating. Maybe Christos would leave Aspasia alone from now on. Perhaps the danger was over.

That thought turned out to be naive as well. My sixth-grade class arrived at three, and we started working on the past tense. Aspasia was sitting outside her room on the top of the stairs, holding two of her dolls and watching us. I was explaining the difference between "drink" and "drank" when someone knocked. Loudly.

"Excuse me." I rose from my stool. My knees started to tremble as I recognized Christos' large form looming in the doorway.

I whipped my head around, and my eyes met Aspasia's. Her face turned pale; she understood. She ran into her room with her dolls and closed the door.

For a moment, I hesitated. If I let Christos in, the children would hear everything. If not, Mrs. D would. But I realized it was a lost cause either way. Christos was so loud that everyone would hear us no matter where we spoke.

I opened the door and stepped outside. Christos stood on the patio in his battered blue captain's hat and decades-old peacoat. I didn't dare glance at Mrs. D, although I felt her staring at us from her bench.

"Where's the child?" Christos demanded. "Why didn't she come?"

"She doesn't want to." I shrugged, as if this puzzled me. "Aspasia decided to play with her dolls. At home."

"The child can do that at my house. Let me see her."

"She's in her room. I don't want to disturb the other children."

Christos narrowed his eyes and stared at me. He's trying to decide if I know, I thought. I kept my expression friendly and innocent. Christos held my gaze for some moments, then his face relaxed. He believed me.

"Tomorrow, then," he said gruffly. "Tell the child I'll buy her a new doll from the store."

"I certainly will."

Christos grunted and walked away, not bothering to close the gate behind him. Mrs. D called out a timid goodbye, which Christos ignored. She tried to catch my eye, but I avoided her and went inside.

Voice shaking, I continued with "drink" and "drank." Aspasia stayed inside her room, not even cracking open the door.

Later when the children were busy scratching in their workbooks, I had a moment to think. Christos would somehow, some way, get to Aspasia again. If she became ill at school or while playing with a friend, people would call me first. But if I were away from home for any of the dozen reasons I might be, they would ask Christos to come get her. Which I wouldn't find out about until I returned from Eleni's or the dentist or wherever I might be.

It was impossible to protect Aspasia absolutely and completely. Christos had violated her once and shattered her in countless ways. If he touched Aspasia again, the shock would compound, the damage multiplying to a point where even my love couldn't reach her.

"Leave," a voice in my head urged. "Pack your bags, cancel your classes, ask Mrs. D to feed the cats. Go stay with friends in Heraklion or Athens. Wait for Dimitris to come home, then go to the police together."

That was the first voice. But a second voice said that even with Dimitris home, nothing would happen. Christos would deny everything, and no punishment would be exacted. It wouldn't bother Christos if Dimitris got angry and stopped talking to him. Christos thought Dimitris was weak-willed and foolish, and he had never respected him.

The second voice also repeated what I had thought earlier. Something had started, and from now on Christos was going to do whatever he could to be alone with Aspasia.

"Either you win or Christos wins," the second voice insisted. "There is no in between."

That evening after I put Aspasia to bed, I lay on the couch under a blanket, reflecting on my situation. A fire crackled in the fireplace, and the gray kitten slept soundly on my stomach.

In my previous life in America, I worked as an assistant to a literary agent. My boss was a kindly man who was training me to eventually co-run the agency. We never imagined I would meet a Greek sailor on the subway to Queens, fall madly in love, and move thousands of miles away.

As I lay on the couch, I recalled eating lunch with my boss and one of our authors at the fancy Manhattan restaurant Café des Artistes. The writer—an anxious man who wrote cozy mysteries set in Brooklyn—was discussing accidental deaths. Apparently the top three were car crashes, falls in the home, and unknowingly ingesting poison.

As I stroked the kitten, I thought about that conversation.

I also remembered something else. An exchange I had with Dimitris shortly after I arrived in Crete.

Following a walk in the mountains, I had developed a rash on my leg. Immediately Dimitris suggested that I rub it with olive oil. In the short time I had been in the village, Dimitris had already managed to recommend olive oil for a slew of problems, bodily as well as culinary.

When he gave me this latest tip, I laughed. "Is there anything you don't use olive oil for?"

Dimitris smiled. "Katerina, this is Crete. We solve all our problems with olive oil."

Sunday

Sunday night.

Five days had passed since Christos raped Aspasia. Through a combination of luck and cunning, I had managed to keep her away from him the entire time.

But that didn't mean Christos had stopped trying.

He didn't return on Thursday after interrupting my class. I had no students on Friday, so Aspasia and I spent the afternoon with Aunt Hara and Yaya. When we came home, we found a new doll propped against our front door. No note, but none was needed. Aspasia didn't say a word as I lifted up the couch cushion and placed the doll in the storage compartment underneath.

On Saturday, Aspasia and I took a walk in the mountains. When we returned, Mrs. D said that Christos had been looking for us.

"He's worried about you," Mrs. D told me eagerly. "You've been acting strange with the child, he says."

Aha, I thought. The rumors were already starting.

"And," Mrs. D went on, "he asked if I had noticed anything odd about you. I told him it was peculiar that you had started walking Aspasia to school. But don't worry, I didn't say anything else."

Was there anything more worthless than Mrs. D's assurance that she hadn't gossiped? I forced a smile and thanked her for letting me know.

Sunday at noon, Christos showed up again. Aspasia had left earlier that morning to spend the day in Sitia with Despina and her family. When I told Christos, his face reddened and he stomped one of his big feet.

"When am I going to see my granddaughter?" he demanded.

"Whenever you like." I kept my expression neutral, painfully aware of Mrs. D sitting on her bench and listening wide-eyed to our exchange. "You know that. But today she's with Despina."

Christos gave a loud snort and walked away. But not before looking over at Mrs. D and shaking his head ominously.

The evidence against me was slowly but steadily mounting. It wouldn't be long before people started calling me a *periptosi*.

My hands shook as I shut my front door. Mrs. D undoubtedly noticed that too.

Sunday night.

A week ago, before this nightmare began, I went to the store to buy chocolate and found Haralambis standing at the counter, flirting playfully with Sophia.

Haralambis was Dimitris' closest friend. In addition to being the best man at our wedding, he was Aspasia's godfather. Tall and slim, he had long legs perpetually clad in jeans and black rubber boots. As usual, his German shepherd Retsina stood by his side, a sweet dog who worshipped him unconditionally.

I remember when Dimitris first introduced me to Haralambis. We shook hands and I smiled, all the while thinking, "Here's trouble." Because Haralambis wasn't just handsome, he was sexy. Typically Greek, with thick wavy black hair, olive complexion, and high cheekbones, he had narrow green eyes and a way of looking at women that you couldn't call lecherous, but you would never call polite.

Haralambis didn't live in our village, but he passed through almost daily on his way to one of his odd jobs. Before Dimitris left, he asked me to have Haralambis over for dinner whenever I could.

"He's shy," Dimitris said. "If you don't ask him, he won't bring it up."

Shy! I didn't think so. Since Dimitris' departure, Haralambis had invited himself to dinner twice. Both times I made sure to have other guests, including some form of available female under age forty. Not that age or availability had ever stopped Haralambis before.

And there he was at the store, cigarettes in hand, leaning on the counter and gazing at Sophia, who was blushing and telling a story with rapid hand gestures. When I entered, Haralambis smiled and gave me one of his frank gazes.

"Here you are!" he said. "Don't you think it's time for another dinner invitation? It's been weeks since I've seen my godchild, and I have a toy rabbit waiting for her."

"When are you free?" I asked.

"Sunday night," he replied. "Let's do it then."

And now it was Sunday night.

With all the horrors of the past week, I had forgotten to invite anyone else. But now I was glad I hadn't. My plan would work better with only one guest.

There was another advantage to having Haralambis at the house. If and when the police were called, he would be the perfect witness. Haralambis loved our family, and he would never betray us. No matter what he saw or suspected.

I was in the middle of cooking dinner when Aspasia raced in after her day in Sitia.

"Is he here?" she called.

"Do you see Retsina?" I replied. "No, so he's not."

Aspasia rushed into the kitchen and wrapped her arms around me, burying her face in my stomach. She was beginning to act like herself again, thank goodness.

"We had fun," she told me. "We went to Despina's cousin's house and we ate *pastitsio* and then we played Barbies. She made her Barbie a singer and mine was an actress, and they lived together in a big house in Athens."

"Is that so?" I said, continuing to cut vegetables. I moved a few steps to get another onion. Aspasia remained glued to me, stepping exactly as I did.

"Then their cat came in, and we played that he was a space monster. He tried to eat my Barbie's hair in the middle of her soap-opera job."

"Is she bald now?"

"No. She hid under a chair so he couldn't get to her."

"That's good. Remember that time on *Lampsi*, when the cat came on the set and ate Virna's hair? It was a disaster."

Aspasia looked up at me. "I don't remember that. You're lying."

"Lying! Me? It was a huge orange cat, don't tell me you forgot about it. He stuck his head in the window when Virna—"

A rapid succession of knocks rang out.

"It's him!" Aspasia cried. She shot into the living room and opened the door. I heard raised voices and laughing and barking.

"Mommy, come see what my godfather brought!"

Wiping my hands on my apron, I walked out of the kitchen. As promised, Haralambis had brought a toy rabbit, but it was too big to fit through the narrow front door. Retsina was already inside and racing around the living room, barking with excitement. Aspasia was as frenzied as the dog, trying to pet Retsina and help her godfather at the same time.

"You told me about the rabbit," I laughed, "but you never said it was bright blue."

"With a gold bow tie," Haralambis added. "Don't forget that."

"Let me help you." I walked over and bent the rabbit's ears. "Now move the tail over a bit . . ."

Haralambis and the rabbit popped through the door. Aspasia threw open her arms, hugging her godfather and the rabbit in one go.

"We're going to have to build another bedroom," I said in a mock scolding tone.

Haralambis winked. "He can sleep with you until Dimitris gets back."

"Ha ha. Excuse me, I have to finish cooking."

In Crete, guests expect to eat right away. I brushed chopped vegetables into the frying pan and poured in olive oil, then added oregano and a pinch of salt and pepper.

"What's for dinner?" Haralambis asked, leaning his long body against the doorframe.

"Spaghetti, your favorite." I had perfected a way of looking at him without actually making eye contact, my glance resting on his face a fraction of a second before skipping off. "Also salad and garlic bread."

"Do you need help?"

"Nope. Go play with Aspasia, she misses you."

"That's not my fault. Nobody invited me."

I waved a hand. "Go."

As the vegetables simmered in oil, I peeked into the living room. Aspasia had dressed the rabbit in one of Dimitris' old sweaters and was trying to stuff his ears into a wool cap.

Kneeling next to her, Haralambis listened attentively as Aspasia explained that the rabbit was off to the North Pole to find his long-lost brother, so he had to dress warmly. The rabbit also needed a guide dog, because he was awfully dumb and might get lost.

Haralambis cheerfully lent out Retsina for the journey and asked what food they should pack.

"Lettuce," Aspasia answered decisively. "Lots of it."

Ducking back into the kitchen, I took a deep breath. I was calm. I had to be.

I stirred tomato sauce in with the oil and chopped vegetables. The spaghetti was already cooked, so I grated cheese into a bowl while the sauce bubbled. Afterward I went into the living room and set the table, pulling it closer to the fireplace so we could eat next to the warmth.

"Food's ready!" I called out.

Aspasia wanted the rabbit to eat with us, so Haralambis set it down on the empty side of the table.

"That's Daddy's place," Aspasia said. "The rabbit can sit there until he comes back."

I had a bad moment then. My throat closed, and tears rose in my eyes. How I wished Dimitris were here! If he were home, none of this would be happening.

Haralambis watched me carefully as I dabbed my eyes with a napkin. Forget about Dimitris, I told myself. He can't help you now.

The moment had arrived. It was time to set my plan in motion.

"Wine?" I asked Haralambis.

He threw open his arms. "Do you even have to ask?"

I went into the kitchen and opened the cabinet under the sink. I pulled out a plastic water bottle filled with wine, then I screwed off the top and sighed loudly.

"We have a problem." I brought the bottle over to Haralambis and held it in front of him. "Look."

He wrinkled his nose. "Flies. Do you have another bottle?"

"No. Not even ordinary wine."

Because this wine was special. Christos had made it, and Haralambis downed at least half a dozen small glasses every time he came to visit.

"This is your fault," he teased. "If you drank yourself, you'd have discovered the flies much earlier."

"Listen," I said, "why don't I run over and get another bottle from Christos? He has plenty."

"You're sure? I would go, but you know how he feels about me."

"That you're a no-good womanizing *malaka*?" I laughed. "I'll grab my coat and head over. It won't take ten minutes."

Aspasia went pale and widened her eyes. As I bent down to give her a hug, I quickly whispered, "Don't worry. *Papoos* won't be coming back with me."

She nodded. I ruffled her hair and smiled.

Still smiling, I took off my apron, slipped on my coat, and went outside. The night sky hung heavy with fog and impending rain.

I turned on my flashlight and glanced across the street. Mrs. D wasn't on her bench, but that didn't mean she wasn't watching.

As I walked to the *kafenio*, I put my hand inside my coat pocket and felt the small bottle of olive oil I had placed there a few hours before. The bottle was sealed with plastic wrap and a rubber band, tightly wedged next to a mitten so it didn't tip over.

Outside the capitalist *kafenio*, I didn't bother to catch my breath or say a final prayer. I pushed down the door handle and walked in, assaulted at once by the distinctive odor of the *kafenio* in winter, a mixture of urine, cleaning fluid, and stale tobacco.

"*Kalispera sas,*" I greeted everyone.

I ran my gaze over the crowded tables until I spied Christos' back. I went over to him and put a hand on his chair. Speaking loudly so everyone could hear, I said, "Christos, excuse me. We've got a dinner guest, and I'm out of your wine."

He frowned. "Already?"

"It's not exactly that I ran out. I didn't close the last bottle very well, and now it's full of flies."

Christos glared at me, then he looked at the others and rolled his eyes. But he was obviously flattered. Making good wine was a matter of pride in Crete, and if I had to pull him away from a game of *prefa* because no other wine would do, that only enhanced his reputation.

He sighed heavily and stubbed out his cigarette. "Kostas, play for me. I'll be back in ten minutes."

"Sorry," I smiled at the other men.

Christos didn't need to put on his hat or coat because, like all the other men in the *kafenio*, he had never taken them off. He rose and strolled to the door with me trailing behind.

A man at another table called out, "Christos, *re*, where are you going?"

He jerked a thumb at me. "She needs wine."

I called out good night and opened the door for Christos to pass through.

Everything had gone smoothly. Exactly as planned.

We stepped out of the *kafenio*. I turned on my flashlight again, and we made a right into the village maze.

"Cold," I commented. "The clouds are sitting on top of the mountains."

"Hmpf." Christos stuck his hands in his pockets and quickened the pace, eager to return to his card game.

I had barely been able to look at him the past week, but now I found myself making small talk. "Were you winning at *prefa?*"

"Who's at your house?" he demanded.

"Haralambis."

"And?"

"Just him. And Aspasia, of course."

"You shouldn't be alone with that man when my son is away. It's not right."

The man who raped my five-year-old daughter was giving me a lecture on morals? Red sizzled up in front of my eyes. I bit my lip a full minute before replying, "Haralambis is Aspasia's godfather."

"He's also slept with half the women in Crete, as well as most of the tourists. What does he want from you?"

"Haralambis had a present for Aspasia. Anyway he's her godfather, and he wanted to see her. What was I supposed to do, say no?"

"You said no to me."

My stomach tensed. "Of course you can see Aspasia whenever you like. This week—I don't know, she felt like staying close to me."

Finally we arrived at Christos' house, and the conversation was thankfully at an end. He pushed open the unlocked door, and we went inside.

The house was neat as a pin, furnished almost exactly like Aunt Hara's but with just a handful of framed photos, no gifts from Dimitris' travels, and far fewer saints. No *mati* charms either. The air smelt as musty as the *kafenio*, as if the windows hadn't been opened in days.

Christos went to the kitchen, and I followed after him. He knelt and rummaged in a cabinet, swearing to himself as he searched. At last he pulled out a plastic motor-oil container and stood up.

"I'll use this," he said. "The top screws on tight, so you won't be wasting any more of my good wine."

I nodded, attempting to look chastened. He grabbed a large funnel off a hook on the wall and went out the front door. The wine was in a storage shed behind the house, which meant Christos would be gone five minutes at most.

Now, I told myself. Now.

I went into the bathroom and turned on the light. I took the bottle of olive oil out of my coat pocket, unhooked the rubber band, and removed the small piece of plastic wrap.

As was common in Crete, the bathroom had only a square porcelain shower base, with no stall or curtain. I knelt down, leaned over the base, and poured out the olive oil. Using my fingertips, I spread the oil until it covered the entire square. The pale golden-green liquid barely showed against the white surface.

I stood and washed my hands. I resealed the bottle with the plastic wrap and rubber band, then put it back in my pocket next to the mitten. I turned off the bathroom light and went into the living room. While I waited for Christos, I circled the room and peered at the sad-eyed saints on the wall.

He came back a few minutes later with the motor-oil container. "*Ela*," he said. "Let's go."

We walked in silence until the cobblestone road forked. Finally Christos handed me the wine.

"Thank you," I said. "Sorry I pulled you away from your game."

He scowled. "I don't want you having that man in your house again, do you hear me? Not when you're alone."

"You're overreacting."

"And I want to see the child tomorrow."

I smiled. "Of course."

Christos went left toward the village center, and I turned right. I kept my mind clear, thinking only that the wine was heavy, the village damp and silent. Also that I was hungry.

Back inside my warm house, the gray kitten was asleep on the rabbit's foot. Aspasia and Haralambis were already eating.

"We couldn't wait," he explained.

"That's OK," I said, handing over the wine.

I hung up my coat, leaving the small bottle tucked in the pocket. Once Haralambis left and Aspasia was in bed, I would take out the bottle, scrub it clean, and put it back in the cupboard.

I stroked Aspasia's hair as I sat down. Home at last.

"Was he angry?" Haralambis asked as he opened up the wine.

"Not at all," I replied, picking up my fork. "You know Christos. He's always willing to help out."

Monday

The next morning, it was raining. Protected by umbrellas—mine large and black, hers small and pink with blue polka dots—Aspasia and I walked to school.

When the wooden doors shut behind her, I stood there for a moment, not ready to be alone. I decided to go to Aunt Hara's house.

As I walked, rain fell steadily, neither heavy nor unpleasant. The moody weather transformed the village and surrounding mountains. Green sweeps of nodding clover glowed as if fluorescent, and the decaying stone houses looked ancient and mysterious in the gray light. I went slowly, past tiny gardens and wrought-iron staircases, past abandoned houses and penned-in animals.

After making a left at the church, I reached Aunt Hara's house. Without knocking, I walked into the living room and was greeted by the familiar sight of Aunt Hara and Yaya sitting on the sofa, working with their hands.

I went to the kitchen and made myself coffee, then returned to the living room and sat down in the armchair. A plate of fresh-baked cookies sat on the table. As I reached out for one, I thought that this was the reason Aunt Hara no longer looked like Aliki Vougiouklaki—too many sweets.

Yaya was picking stems off raisins, and Aunt Hara was busy knitting a pullover.

"Who's the sweater for?" I asked.

Aunt Hara and Yaya exchanged murderous glances.

"Never mind," I laughed. "If it's going to start a fight, I'd rather not know."

One of the weekly television guides was next to the plate of cookies. I picked it up and spread it open on my knees.

"Page ten," Yaya told me.

Aunt Hara sighed in exasperation, but I felt I had no choice. I turned to page ten, and there was Virna from *Lampsi*, wearing a striped dress and smiling broadly. She was sitting with a woman with black-framed glasses, the author of the play in Athens that Virna was currently starring in.

"She's tall," I commented. "And she looks much younger without makeup."

"It would be nice to see the play," Yaya said.

Aunt Hara's silence was as sharp as a knife. I made sure to spend an appropriate amount of time staring at the photograph, then I discreetly turned the page. While I sipped coffee and ate another cookie, I read an interview with the actress Mimi Denissi, occasionally wiping crumbs off the guide.

Then I wasn't reading at all. Instead I was thinking about Christos. A few years before, he had complained about stiffness in his shoulders, and I told him that a hot shower daily rather than once a week would ease the pain. Christos had scorned this frivolous luxury, but about a month later he grudgingly admitted that showering every day really did help.

So this morning, Christos had tumbled out of bed and flicked the switch in the fuse box. He puttered around the house while the water heated, then took off his clothes in the bedroom and went naked into the bathroom.

What next?

Maybe Christos had decided, for whatever reason, not to shower today. He could be sitting at the *kafenio* right now, drinking coffee and thinking about my daughter.

Or Christos did take a shower. He put one foot in the porcelain square and felt himself starting to slide. Immediately he reached out and grabbed the sink to steady himself. When Christos touched the square to see why he had slipped, he was puzzled to find a thin layer of olive oil.

Perhaps Christos did fall and injure himself. There was such a range of possibilities if he had. Light bruising or a complicated break? A mild concussion or a sharp crack on the back of the head?

Death was the goal. But any injury would be welcome, particularly if it limited Christos' mobility. Anything at all that could buy Aspasia and me a little time.

Of course, if Christos actually died, I would have other problems.

When Eleni's husband fell out of the olive tree, an ambulance came and so did the police. They didn't suspect foul play, but there was a dead body, and dead bodies required the authorities. Not that anything dramatic occurred once the two officers arrived. They asked a few questions, jotted the answers in their notebooks, then retired to the *kafenio* to drink *raki*.

Hopefully no one would suspect anything if Christos died. But I had read enough detective novels to realize the obvious questions. How did the olive oil get into the bathroom? If Christos had brought it in, why was there no bottle or glass? And if he had rubbed the olive oil into his skin or hair, why wasn't there any on his hands?

At least the olive oil belonged to Christos. He had given me a barrel recently and that's what I used, making it impossible to prove the oil in the bathroom was from my house. To an American like me, all olive oil looked the same. But this was Crete, and I had heard enough discussions to know that it was as easy to identify as wine.

It was true that everyone in the *kafenio*, as well as Haralambis, knew I'd been in Christos' house on Sunday evening. But so what? No one had seen the bottle of oil in my pocket, and no one had witnessed me pouring it into the shower base.

My best alibi was my wholesome life. I was Dimitris' wife and Aspasia's mother, and I taught English to most of the village children. Fortunately, Christos' gossip campaign against me was in its infancy, so I wasn't yet considered a *periptosi*.

The only thing that could ever condemn me was my own confession, and that would never happen. I knew why I did it and I didn't feel guilty, so I had no need to unburden myself.

Even so, I wish I knew if Christos had fallen. And if he were alive. Or preferably dead.

"**A**ny more news from Dimitris?" Yaya asked.

"No," I sighed. "Nothing."

"I plan to write him a letter tonight. There's something he needs to know."

Aunt Hara paused her knitting. "You're going to bother him about that play, aren't you? Don't you dare try to make him feel guilty."

"I'm old and I'm about to die. The only thing I want to do before I leave this earth is see that play."

Aunt Hara rolled her eyes. "Excuse me. I keep forgetting you're dying."

"I am, just you wait and see. My time is running out." Once again Yaya made her favorite gesture, closing her eyes and leaning her head against her palm. "You'll be sorry the rest of your life that you didn't take me."

Aunt Hara was unperturbed. "If you go to Athens, you might fall off a curb or get hit by a car. It's dangerous there."

"Fine, then I'll die happy."

I was about to inject a sorely needed dose of sanity when someone pounded on the door.

"Come in," Aunt Hara called.

The door flew open. Sophia's father stood in the doorway, one hand on his heaving chest, his hair soaked from the rain.

"Sophia said you'd all be here. Come, it's Christos! There's been an accident."

Aunt Hara turned white and made a choking noise. Yaya crossed herself and said, "Dear God."

"Elate!" Sophia's father beckoned. "Come!"

I sat motionless in the armchair. I tried to inhale, but my breath felt stuck.

Yaya shook the raisins off the scarf and onto the table, then tied the scarf on her head. She put a hand on my arm. "I've buried four grandparents, my own parents, my husband, my in-laws, one child, and more cousins than you can count. You get used to it. So *ela*, let's go."

I rose and put on my coat, then found my umbrella by the door. Aunt Hara followed behind me and wrestled on an old-fashioned black trench coat that smelled of mothballs. As she wrapped a black scarf around her head, I saw that her eyes were full of tears.

The rain had turned heavy, a relentless downpour of cold, sharp drops. Yaya, for all her imagined ill health, ran ahead of both Aunt Hara and me. She drew alongside Sophia's father, then passed him too.

We turned left and then right through a short alley, took a left and another right, and there was Christos' house. The front door was open, and a crowd of villagers was trying to press inside.

Aunt Hara and I stepped onto the concrete patio, but we couldn't move past the throng. It seemed everyone from the *kafenia* had come, bringing that stale smell with them. I stood on tiptoe and saw that Yaya had managed to squeeze in, her black headscarf weaving through the crowd.

A prickly sensation ran through my chest. What if they all knew? Maybe this was a trap and everyone was watching me, waiting for me to make a slip.

Someone on my left laid a sympathetic hand on my arm. I turned to look at the woman, my throat thickening until I could hardly breathe.

"Elate!" someone shouted. "Hara and Katerina are here, let them pass!"

After more shouting, the crowd finally stirred, and a great fuss ensued. A few people tried to back up while others pushed forward, leaving everyone stuck.

"Go into the bedroom!" someone cried.

As soon as the bedroom door opened, part of the crowd moved in there. Aunt Hara took my elbow, and we walked through the concerned faces and wringing hands.

One of Christos' card-playing cronies, a short man with bushy gray eyebrows, stood blocking the bathroom doorway.

"He's still alive," he told us. "I felt a pulse. I'm making sure no one touches him before the ambulance arrives."

"What happened?" Aunt Hara asked, her voice trembling.

The man shrugged. "Christos didn't come to the *kafenio* this morning. We didn't think much of it, but when we needed a third for *prefa*, I went to look for him.

"No one answered when I knocked, so I opened the door and found him here. Looks like he fell and hit his head." The man winced. "Actually, his face."

Aunt Hara let out a tortured sob and crossed herself.

Say something, I scolded myself. Act normal. "Who called the ambulance?" I finally squeaked out.

"Sophia," the man told me. "After I found Christos, I ran back to the *kafenio*. I saw Sophia as I was about to go in, and I asked her to call."

"Which means they'll be here in a half hour," Aunt Hara sighed. "If they can find the house."

"Sophia is waiting by the main road," he replied. "She'll lead them here."

"Can we see him?" I asked.

Christos' friend stepped away. At first all I saw was Yaya's tiny black figure kneeling by the porcelain square, her elbow jabbing repeatedly as she crossed herself.

I shifted slightly to the left. Behind me, Aunt Hara let out a squeal. Now we could see Christos. He was naked and lying face down across the shower base. A pool of blood seeped from both sides of his head.

Christos must have stepped into the shower and lost his footing. Then he fell to the floor and smashed his face on the edge of the base.

"Careful," I said to Yaya, kneeling beside her and pulling away her black skirt. "There's blood."

Yaya nodded and moved back a bit. I put my arm around her and stared at the porcelain square. Even from this close, the oil wasn't obvious. Christos' fall appeared to be an accident, and from the bits of conversation I could hear, no one thought differently.

They don't know, I thought. And they don't suspect a thing.

The prickly feeling dissolved. A few moments later, I was able to take a full breath.

The police would surely be arriving soon, although no one had mentioned them. I wanted to ask if someone had called the station, but decided against it. I had to be careful not to say too much. Above all, I had to act normal.

And what was normal? For an American like me, normal meant biting my lip and keeping my feelings inside. But this was Greece, and emotions were flowing freely. The women wailed, and many men wept openly into rusty handkerchiefs. Even Aunt Hara, who never had a kind word for Christos, blubbered quietly.

Yaya remained calm, saying her prayers and crossing herself. Suddenly she stopped and took my arm. "Someone has to go with Christos to the hospital."

"Not me," I replied at once. "I need to be here when Aspasia gets out of school. I want to be the one to tell her what happened."

"And I'm too damn old." Yaya got to her feet, and I followed. "Hara," she said sternly. "Pull yourself together. You have to go to the hospital with Christos."

"In the ambulance?" Aunt Hara whimpered.

"That's right. Katerina will wait to speak to Aspasia, then she'll drive over and meet you there."

The last thing I wanted to do was cancel my classes and sit with Christos. But it would look strange if I didn't.

"OK," I agreed. "But who'll watch Aspasia while I'm gone?"

"I will," Yaya replied.

"Dimitris," I said suddenly.

"What can poor Dimitris do? He's in the middle of the Pacific Ocean."

I sighed. "Not even the middle, unfortunately."

A roar went up from the crowd: the ambulance had arrived.

Sophia marched into the house. *"Elate!"* she shouted. "They can't come inside because there's too many people."

She yelled a few more times until everyone finally got the message and began to leave. I ducked into the kitchen with Aunt Hara and Yaya, waiting for the rooms to empty.

Two young orderlies with stained white smocks carried a wooden stretcher into the living room. Behind them was an older man in an equally dirty smock, holding a black bag and a dripping umbrella.

"I'm the doctor," he announced. "Where's the patient?"

"In the bathroom," Yaya said, pointing at the door.

The doctor hurried past us and went into the bathroom. We moved over to the doorway and peered in, watching as he knelt down and took Christos' pulse. Next he put both hands under Christos' head and lifted it off the floor.

Whatever the doctor saw made him cluck his tongue. He stood and wiped his hands on his smock, shaking his head solemnly.

"It's not good." He motioned to the orderlies. "One of you go in and lift him by the shoulders, the other one needs to stand in the doorway and get his feet. Whatever you do, don't let the head fall."

An orderly went into the bathroom and planted a foot in the shower base. Oh God! What if he slipped on the oil too? I nearly called out, but stopped myself. I watched as the young man straddled Christos, then bent down and grabbed him by the shoulders.

"Step back," Sophia told us. "They can't do their job."

With one arm around Aunt Hara's shoulders, she led us into the living room.

"How can I go to the hospital?" Aunt Hara wept. "My purse is at home, and I don't have any money."

"I'll bring your purse when I come this afternoon," I said.

"And I have money." Sophia reached into her bra and pulled out a wad of cash. "Here, take ten thousand drachmas."

"You'll come soon?" Aunt Hara asked, clutching my hand.

"As soon as I can," I promised.

The orderlies had lifted Christos and were carrying him to the stretcher. Then, with a movement not as gentle as it might have been, they rotated Christos so he was face up.

I gasped and Aunt Hara screamed. Christos' face was purple and distended. His forehead was split open, and his nose was smashed to one side. He must have hit the edge of the shower base at the worst possible angle.

My eyes moved down his body to check for other injuries. At the site of his flaccid penis, I turned my head away in disgust.

The orderlies covered Christos with a blanket and fashioned a headrest out of towels. They each took an end of the stretcher, then counted to three and hoisted it off the ground.

The doctor directed them out the door. We were about to follow when Sophia pointed to a trail of blood leading from the bathroom to the living room.

Yaya looked at the blood, then me. "As soon as the ambulance goes, we need to come back and clean up."

In other words, wipe up the porcelain shower base and the oil. Erase the evidence. My heart lightened, and I had to suppress a hysterical laugh.

"Yes," I said, linking my arm in hers. "Good idea."

Rain fell hard and steady. The doctor called out something to the villagers gathered in front of the house. A man stepped forward to open the doctor's umbrella and hold it over Christos' head.

The crowd went first, then the stretcher. We followed behind, with Sophia and Aunt Hara beneath one umbrella, Yaya and I under another. The sweet thick smell of moist earth filled the air; a goat bleated from one of the animal stalls, and another goat answered.

The orderlies made it up the first lane. As they rounded the corner, the orderly in back slipped and fell on the wet cobblestones. He dropped his end of the stretcher, whereupon Christos started sliding off. The doctor cursed, and several women screamed and crossed themselves furiously. I clutched the handle of my umbrella, unable to move.

The other orderly laid down his end of the stretcher, and a few of the villagers helped him reposition Christos. The two orderlies were about to pick up the stretcher again when, in a move typically Cretan, two of the villagers shoved the orderlies aside, grabbed the handles, and shouted, "Let's go!"

The procession twisted and turned through the narrow streets. Finally we reached the village center. The back of the ambulance was open, with the driver leaning against the door, cigarette in hand. The orderlies secured Christos, then the doctor climbed in and huddled over him, swabbing at his face and shouting for bandages.

Yaya exchanged a few words with the driver. He opened the passenger door and motioned Aunt Hara to get in. When she hesitated, Yaya and I leaned into her, using our weight to push her into the seat.

I propped my umbrella over the open door, then Yaya and I pressed in so Aunt Hara couldn't leave. She was still crying, wringing her hands and clutching her handkerchief.

"Pull yourself together," Yaya commanded. "Crying won't help."

"You'll come soon?" Aunt Hara asked me again.

"As soon as I can," I repeated.

"Make sure you clean up. The blood will stain if you don't wipe it up now."

"Don't worry," I assured her. "We will."

The doors in back slammed shut. I kissed Aunt Hara on both cheeks and shut her door. The driver turned on the engine, and the red-and-blue lights on top began revolving. I waved at Aunt Hara's panicked face as they pulled away.

When the ambulance hit the main road, the driver turned on the siren and sped away. The sound of the retreating wail hung in the air, then disappeared into the mist.

Yaya and I stood in the village center under my umbrella. She tugged my sleeve.

"Let's go back to the house," she said. "Before the blood dries."

Everyone else started to disappear into their homes and the *kafenia*, but not before stopping to offer help and condolences. This was the best part of village life. People were always willing to lend a hand, and even enemies set aside their grudges when misfortune struck.

Never mind that I was the one who'd set this particular bad luck in motion.

That's not true, I told myself as Yaya and I walked arm in arm on the slippery cobblestones. Christos started all this, and he was the one to blame. Anyone who raped a child had to expect consequences.

And how was I feeling now that my plan had worked out so well? I didn't feel guilty, that was certain. Still, the thought of being alone filled me with panic, and it was comforting to be with Yaya. Her belief that Christos' fall was an accident helped me forget that it was not.

Again I wondered about the police. Why hadn't they come?

Suddenly I realized that the police wouldn't be coming. No one had called them because no one had died. And except for me, no one knew that a crime had been committed.

The thought made me so relieved I almost laughed aloud. Again.

The front door of Christos' house stood wide open. Yaya went in first while I paused on the patio and shook off my umbrella.

Inside it was dim and shadowy from the leaden sky, so we quickly turned on all the lights. An eerie quiet filled the empty rooms.

"I'll take the bathroom, and you do the living room," Yaya said, flipping on the switch for the hot-water heater.

"Let me do the bathroom," I offered quickly. "It's too much work for you."

"I don't mind."

Yaya went into the kitchen and rummaged through the cabinets. She filled two plastic buckets with hot soapy water, then handed one to me along with some rags.

"Seriously, Yaya, I'd rather do the bathroom. You—"

But she was already on her way out of the kitchen.

My heart beat faster. Nothing to do but clean up the living room. If I made any more of a fuss, it would seem odd. The worst thing I could do was act strange, even if it was just in front of Yaya.

The blood had been bright when it fell, but it had already turned a few shades darker. I wiped the thick line of drops with a soapy rag, then dried the floor with another. A few drops had managed to splash onto the table and under the couch, so I cleaned them away too.

"Done," I called out.

I went to the bathroom and stood in the doorway. Yaya was on her knees, furiously scrubbing the tile floor with a wooden brush. The large patches of blood were gone, but red had seeped into the seams between the tiles and was deeply ingrained.

"*Ela*, Yaya!" I protested. "Let me do that. You don't have to spend all morning on the floor."

She rocked back on her heels. "If you're sure . . ."

"My turn," I shooed her out.

Yaya handed me the brush, but she didn't leave. Instead she sat on the toilet, watching as I got on my knees and started scouring the shower base.

Suddenly Yaya leaned over and touched the porcelain square. She raised her finger to the light and stared at it with a frown.

"Strange," she mused. "There's olive oil here."

My breath froze.

"Really?" I asked, not looking up.

She sniffed her finger. "I'm sure of it. Feel." She held her hand in front of my face.

I reached out and lightly brushed Yaya's gnarled finger, which was now slick with oil.

"That must be why he slipped," she said. "How peculiar."

I turned back to the shower base and scrubbed with all my might, gritting my teeth to stop myself from saying one single word. The absolute best thing I could do now was to make sure all the oil—all the evidence—disappeared.

There was, however, one place I couldn't scrub clean, namely Yaya's sharp mind with its prodigious memory.

Yaya knew. And she would not forget.

After the shower base was clean and dried, I scrubbed the tiles for a solid ten minutes. When all the blood was gone, I gave the floor a final fierce swipe. Hands shaking, I took the bucket into the kitchen to throw out the bloody water.

Yaya followed me and watched as I worked. "Maybe Christos needs some things in the hospital," she said. "Should I pack a bag?"

"Good idea," I replied. "I'll bring it when I go."

"Don't bother rinsing out those rags or that brush, just throw them away. While you're at it, get rid of the food and garbage. Who knows how long this place will be closed up."

I was tempted to ask Yaya if she thought Christos was going to die, but I stopped myself.

Under the sink, I found a large garbage bag and stuffed the rags and brush inside. I wanted to toss out the buckets as well, but Yaya said Christos would be angry if I did. Mostly because he was too cheap to buy new ones, and also because the blood was his own so it wouldn't bother him.

There was a loaf of bread and hunk of cheese sitting on the counter, so I threw them away. In the refrigerator I found wilted vegetables, a plate of *pastitsio*, an expired can of condensed milk, and a bowl with a half dozen eggs. I threw out everything except the eggs.

"I'll take those," Yaya said, coming in with a small suitcase. "And you should unplug the refrigerator."

"You think that's necessary?" I asked.

"I saw Christos' face. He won't be coming back here any time soon."

I wrapped the eggs in newspaper and handed the packet to Yaya, who nestled it in her roomy apron. Then I went into the bathroom to empty the wastebasket. Before I turned out the light, I looked around carefully. No oil anywhere.

Yaya and I left the house. I put the garbage bag in the corner of the concrete patio, and we had a discussion about locking the door. If there was a key, we didn't know where it was. Not that it mattered; there was nothing much to steal, and anyway no one would.

The thought of separating from Yaya made me nervous, so as we walked under my umbrella I said, "Why don't you get your crocheting and stay at my house until I pick up Aspasia? You don't have to be alone."

Yaya looked at me and nodded. "I'd like that."

"This afternoon when I'm at the hospital, you can teach Aspasia to crochet. She's been dying to learn."

We stopped at Aunt Hara's so Yaya could pick up a dry scarf and her sewing bag. Halfway back to my house, Yaya stopped in her tracks. "Why was there olive oil in the shower?"

Once again, my breath froze. It took a moment to realize that Yaya was asking a rhetorical question. She didn't actually expect me to have the answer.

"I don't know," I stammered. "Do you think Christos used it in his hair?"

"Maybe," she said thoughtfully. "Maybe."

Due to the rain, Mrs. D was not on her bench. But as soon as Yaya and I arrived at my house, Mrs. D poked her head out the front door.

Yaya drew in a sharp breath. She didn't like Mrs. D.

"Oh, poor Christos!" Mrs. D cried. "I heard all about it. Where is he?"

"In the ambulance," I replied. "He's going to the hospital in Sitia. Aunt Hara is with him."

"Come inside! I'll fix coffee and you can tell me everything."

I put on a regretful smile. "That's kind of you, but I have to make some phone calls."

"Are you going to the hospital?" she asked, eyes alight with excitement.

"As soon as Aspasia comes home from school."

"Poor little thing, she loves her *papoos* so much! Will Antigone be staying with you?"

I had nearly forgotten that Yaya's name was Antigone. "Yes, she'll be here all day." I looked over at Yaya. She had already crossed the patio and was opening the front door.

"Let me know as soon as there's news," Mrs. D said. "And tell Antigone she's welcome to visit. We haven't talked in ages."

"I'll let her know."

When I entered the house, Yaya was standing in the center of the living room, hands on her hips.

"That witch! She tried to steal my husband when we first started courting, and now she has the nerve to be friendly."

"Shh!" I laughed. "Mrs. D has very good hearing."

"I don't care."

"She wants you to come over."

"Not in a thousand years. My, that's a very large rabbit."

Yaya sat in the kitchen while I fixed coffee. She offered to cook lunch, and I suggested we eat lentils. We moved into the living room, where I lit a fire and brought Yaya a pile of lentils to clean. I sat by the phone and started making calls.

"*Ya soo*, it's Katerina. There won't be any class today. I don't know if you've heard, but my father-in-law is in the hospital."

That was me, acting normal.

I waited for Aspasia in front of the school. The rain had stopped, but the sky was the color of steel, and I had my umbrella tucked under my arm just in case.

I wasn't sure how Aspasia would react to the news about her *papoos*. Ever since Christos attacked her, she'd had good moments and bad. She would seem completely fine for hours, only to suddenly deflate, her eyes dimming and her face growing sad. At those moments, I took Aspasia in my arms and held her tight, loving her back to life.

The bell rang. The wooden doors opened, and the children poured out. Aspasia ran straight into my arms, still elated from Haralambis' visit and the bright-blue rabbit. I gave her a hug, then she took my hand and we started walking home.

We were just past the church when I said, "Let's go over to the lookout and sit for a minute."

Aspasia glanced up at me. "Everything's wet."

"We can sit on my rain slicker. *Ela*, just for a moment."

The lookout—just a bench behind a wooden rail—had a stunning view of the interlocking valleys that stretched down to the sea. With the mist and vibrant green colors, it looked like something out of a fairy tale.

I took off my rain slicker and sat on it, gently drawing Aspasia down next to me. Judging from the wall of clouds moving toward us, I didn't have much time.

"I have something to tell you," I began. "It's sad, but it's also a relief."

"What?"

"Today when your *papoos* was going into the shower, he slipped and hit his head. He's in the hospital now."

"Is he sick?"

"Very. And he might die. That's sad. But the good part is, we don't have to be scared anymore. Your *papoos* won't be bothering you again."

Aspasia said nothing.

"Yaya is at our house because Aunt Hara went to the hospital. After we eat lunch, I'm going there too."

Aspasia looked at me fearfully. I lay my hand on her cheek. "You don't have to worry anymore, honey. Your *papoos* isn't here."

"When will you come back?"

"In the evening."

"Are you just going today?"

I sighed. "I might have to be there a lot now. But let's see. I don't know how long this will last."

"Did Yaya see my rabbit?"

"She did, and she was very impressed."

We left the lookout and walked home. Just before we turned into our street, I stopped and knelt in front of Aspasia. I wanted to ask her not to tell Yaya what Christos had done, but I needed to do so without scaring or threatening her.

I was about to speak when Aspasia put a hand on my shoulder. "Don't worry, Mommy. I won't say anything to Yaya about what happened. But when Daddy comes home, can we tell him?"

"Yes," I said. "Of course we will."

"OK."

I closed my eyes and laid my chin on top of her little head.

The pale-green hospital hallway stretched out long and narrow, lit by flickering fluorescent lights. As I walked toward the far end, I glanced into the rooms. From the mute eyes and wasted limbs, I could tell this was the ward where people came to die.

I found Aunt Hara sitting on a bench outside one of the rooms, crying noisily into a handkerchief.

"Katerina!" Aunt Hara rose and gave me a hug. "Thank God! The doctors are with him now, they asked me to wait out here."

I hugged her back, then we both sat. "Any news?"

She shook her head. "Not really. I don't know."

I sighed and took her hand. Obviously Aunt Hara had been the wrong person to send. I never knew what to expect from her—she could be cold and hard, but also weakly sentimental. Aunt Hara hated Christos, yet here she was crying as if Dimitris or Yaya lay inside the room.

"I wish I was back in the village," she said mournfully. "How's *mama*?"

"Yaya's fine. She cleaned all my lentils, and this afternoon she's going to teach Aspasia how to crochet."

"Good," Aunt Hara said between sniffs. "She's the perfect age to start. Did you tell Aspasia about Christos?"

"I did. She was sad, but I think she's too young to really understand."

"Perhaps that's best."

The door to Christos' room opened. Two doctors came out, a middle-aged man carrying a chart, and a clean-cut man younger than me.

After greeting us hastily, the young doctor hurried down the hall. The other one looked at his chart, then me. "You're—?"

"Katerina Theodorakis. His daughter-in-law."

"I'm Dr. Petrakis. Wait here, I'll get a chair."

He shambled down the hall, and as he came back I had a good look at him. With his ashy skin, bloodshot eyes, and listless gait, he was one of the unhealthiest-looking people I had ever seen. If he hadn't been wearing a white coat, I would have thought he was a patient.

The doctor opened the window above the bench. He sat down on his chair wearily, then lit a cigarette and took a long, hard drag.

"How is he?" I asked.

"Not good," the doctor said, blowing smoke out the window. "Your father-in-law took a hard knock and he's unconscious. Blows to the head aren't always this serious, but he landed badly. I don't know if he'll wake up."

"So—"

"He might die in an hour, a few weeks, even a year. Or he could wake up. But we can't discount brain damage, so maybe it's better he doesn't regain consciousness."

Aunt Hara moaned, and I put a hand on her knee.

"Do you want a cigarette?" the doctor asked me.

"No, thanks."

"Give me one," Aunt Hara said.

I raised my eyebrows. "You don't smoke!"

"I do in hospitals."

The doctor handed Aunt Hara a lit cigarette, and she inhaled shakily.

"So what's next?" I asked.

"We watch him," the doctor replied. "He's not bleeding internally, as far as I can tell. But it's a bad sign that he's unconscious. He looks like a strong man, though, so maybe he'll wake up and be fine."

"OK," I said uncertainly.

"I'll be checking on him throughout the day, but otherwise there's nothing we can do." The doctor tilted his head and looked at me. "Will your husband be coming soon? I'd like to talk to him."

My heart sank. "Dimitris is working as an electrician on a cargo ship. He left Japan about a week ago."

"I wouldn't bother trying to contact him at this point, since we don't have any definitive news. Where's he going?"

"San Diego. He should arrive in about three weeks. Maybe more, depending on the weather."

"I love the sea," the doctor declared wistfully. "I have a boat at the harbor, I go fishing whenever I can."

He asked me about Dimitris' responsibilities on the ship. I answered as best I could, all the while expecting the conversation to return to Christos. But it was as if the doctor had forgotten him altogether.

When a nurse passed by, the doctor asked if she would run out and buy us coffee. Cheese pies too, did we want any? The bakery across the street made them fresh.

The coffee and cheese pies came. As the doctor was confessing his unfulfilled dream of sailing around the world, I interrupted him. "Are we keeping you from something?"

"Not at all. Tell me, does your husband make a good living? My daughter's boyfriend is an electrician, and I'm afraid if they get married, he won't be able to support her."

Down the hall, a door opened and a nurse stuck her head out. "Doctor!" she called. "Come quickly, we have a problem."

He sighed and stubbed out his cigarette on the windowsill. "We'll talk more later." With that, he rose sluggishly and slumped off toward his duties.

"I suppose we should see Christos now," Aunt Hara said.

I took a deep breath. "Let's go."

We rose off the bench. Aunt Hara nodded, and I pulled open the door.

The room had two beds separated by a cracked beige screen. From behind the screen came voices and the smell of food.

"Another family," Aunt Hara murmured. "Here's Christos. Oh, I'm afraid to see!"

So was I, but there was no avoiding it. I turned my head and looked down at the bed.

Hot panic shot through me. Christos was staring at me, he was awake!

It took a moment to realize that only one of his cold green eyes was open, frozen in place. The other was shut tight and covered with swollen purple skin.

Aunt Hara crossed herself several times and murmured a prayer. When she was finished, I handed her the assortment of silver icons and *mati* charms that Yaya had gathered from their house.

As Aunt Hara arranged everything around Christos' bed, I edged closer to get a better look at him. His head was heavily bandaged, and his left temple was caved in. Tubes protruded from his nose and arms, and a monitor next to the bed beeped as wrinkled green lines strolled across the screen.

After being afraid of Christos for so long, I could hardly believe he was now just a helpless old man in a hospital bed. I kept expecting him to rise up and bark out an insult. But no, he was as still as a stone.

"I just realized something," I said, turning to Aunt Hara. "That doctor didn't tell us anything. One moment he says there's no hope, that even if Christos does regain consciousness, there might be brain damage. Then he says Christos is strong and might wake up any moment with no problems at all."

"That's just how the doctor is."

But it wasn't Aunt Hara who answered. The beige screen was now folded back a little, and a plump woman with crossed eyes was standing in the gap. She held out a tin box with wedges of yellow cake.

"*Elate,*" she said in a friendly voice. "Have some."

Aunt Hara glanced at me. I could tell she was struggling, unsure if it was proper to indulge while Christos lay so close to death.

As always, Aunt Hara's sweet tooth won out. She went over to the woman and took two pieces.

"You need napkins," the cross-eyed woman said. "Just a moment."

She folded back the screen completely, revealing four more people. They were sitting around a man who was just skin and bones, full of tubes and attached to his own slowly beeping monitor.

In Greece, it's traditional for families to stay around the clock if someone is hospitalized, but these people were entrenched. Each folding chair had a cushion, and a small television sat on the bedside table. The broad windowsill held foil-covered platters, a loaf of bread on a cutting board, and a portable gas burner with a *briki*. Two women were crocheting, one man was reading a book, and the other fingered thick amber worry beads.

The cross-eyed woman went over to the buffet and plucked out two napkins. Everyone else stared at us with friendly curiosity.

"It's not that I don't like the doctor," the cross-eyed woman continued, "but he never gives a straight answer. *Elate*, bring those folding chairs over here. When the screen's pulled back, there's enough space between the beds. An old woman was here before your poor man, and sometimes we fit twelve people."

Aunt Hara and I moved two chairs between the beds as instructed. I wouldn't have been surprised if the cross-eyed woman had taken out a deck of cards and suggested a round of *prefa*.

We set up our chairs so they faced away from Christos. As we ate the cake, Aunt Hara kept turning around to check on him.

"We'll let you know if he twitches or something," the cross-eyed woman said. "My name is Elektra."

"I'm Katerina," I said. "And this is Hara."

"Nice to meet you. This is my sister, Clytemnestra," she continued. "These are my brothers, Pericles and Leonidas. And this is Leonidas' wife, Zoe."

The last name was announced with distaste; the sister-in-law was clearly not a favorite.

"Our father—that's him in the bed—he gave us all ancient names. He loved Greek history."

"My daughter is Aspasia," I told her.

Aunt Hara glared at me. Were we really going to socialize with these people? But I didn't think we had a choice.

"A beautiful name," Elektra beamed. "You have an accent, are you Greek?"

"I'm from America."

"Are your parents Greek?"

"No, not at all."

This made me very interesting. While Zoe fixed us coffee, Elektra plied me with questions. Before long she had extracted my life story, with the other family members chiming in whenever my history overlapped with theirs. Pericles had traveled on cargo ships in his youth, Clytemnestra's daughter taught at a *frondistirio* in Chania, and Leonidas had a friend in our village. Aunt Hara took another piece of cake, and I might have forgotten where I was if their father hadn't suddenly defecated.

"Oh my," Aunt Hara said.

"You'll get used to it," Elektra assured her. "I'll show you how we do it."

"Isn't that the nurses' job?" I asked faintly. "I'll run out in the hall and find one."

"Don't bother. He's our father, we'll do it."

They put down their books and crocheting and worry beads. With quiet efficiency, they rolled the old man onto his side and removed the dirty nightshirt. Elcktra wiped his bottom, and I wrinkled my nose as the smell of feces filled the room.

Aunt Hara started to cross herself, but before she could even finish, their father was wearing a clean nightshirt, and Clytemnestra was out the door with the soiled laundry. Pericles opened the window to disperse the smell, then they all sat down and picked up their various activities.

"How long have you been here?" Aunt Hara asked.

"Five months," Elektra replied.

Aunt Hara and I glanced at each other.

"I need to talk to you," she whispered. "Alone."

Aunt Hara and I set down our coffee. We rose and told the others we'd be back in a moment.

I closed the door behind us, and we stood in the pale-green hallway. Aunt Hara put her hands on her hips and looked at me steely-eyed. The old man's bowel movement had thoroughly banished her sentimental tears.

"If you don't mind," she told me, "I'm getting the bus back to the village. I'm going to phone every relative Christos has and make them promise to come here. This can't all fall on us. You and I aren't related to Christos by blood, and we don't even like him."

I opened my mouth to protest, but Aunt Hara held up a hand. "Don't say a word. I'll come every day and so will you, but Christos is not our responsibility, or not ours alone." She pursed her lips. "I wish Dimitris were here. Eleni won't help us, and Stamatina—"

"Forget about her," I cut in. "But at least call so she knows what's going on."

"All right. Then I'll contact everyone else I can. And I won't take no for an answer."

Aunt Hara ducked into Christos' room and grabbed her purse and coat. We kissed each other's cheeks, and she hugged me so tightly my nose got lost in her puffy brown hair.

"You're a good girl," she said. "I'm glad Dimitris married you."

Aunt Hara bustled down the hallway, clearly relieved to be leaving Christos and the cheerful family with the ancient names. She pushed the double doors open and disappeared from my sight. The doors flapped vigorously before slowly coming to a stop.

I knew I should go back into the room to keep watch over Christos, but instead I sat down on the bench and took several long, deep breaths.

OK, I told myself. The worst is behind you. Or at least this part is behind you.

At the end of the hallway, the doors swished open. I looked up, expecting to see a nurse or the unhealthy doctor, but it was someone else entirely.

A policeman.

The policeman walked slowly, his head swiveling as he glanced at the room numbers.

He's looking for me, I thought. That's why he's here.

What had gone wrong? It must have been Yaya. She figured out what I'd done, and she turned me in.

No, she would never do that! If Yaya suspected something, she would talk to me first. She wouldn't risk getting me in trouble and leaving Aspasia without a mother.

Had anybody seen me? Someone who silently came into Christos' house while I poured the oil? No, that was impossible, I would have heard them.

Perhaps Aspasia confided in her teacher about what Christos had done. The teacher put the pieces together and went to the police, and now it was just a matter of my confession.

Which I won't give, I thought wildly. I won't!

Did Haralambis tell on me? Maybe when he was hanging up his leather jacket, he bumped against my coat and felt something hard. That's when he looked in my pocket and saw the bottle filled with olive oil. Haralambis mentioned it to someone, and when they figured out what the oil was for, they called the police.

The policeman moved slowly toward me. My brain spun colors and my mouth filled with dust. The impulse to flee was excruciating. I pressed my trembling hands on my legs to stop from bolting.

He continued his leisurely stroll, head moving from side to side as his glance bounced off the room numbers. Step by step, room by room, the policeman worked his way down the hallway.

If the police had indisputable proof I'd somehow overlooked, I could tell them what Christos had done to Aspasia. But only if they had proof. And what could that possibly be? I had been so careful!

Step by step. Closer now, I saw the policeman's tight collar, his dark curly hair and narrow eyes. He was so close I could smell his aftershave, a heavy musk that covered the rotten odor of sick people.

He stopped in front of me. I raised my head and looked him in the eye.

"Yes?" I said too loudly.

He grinned. "I think I'm lost. My *yaya* is in room 354, but I only see odd numbers. There must be another hall parallel to this one."

"I don't know," I replied. "Today is the first time I've ever been here."

"You're foreign. Where are you from, Germany?"

"America."

"I have relatives there, in Queens. As does half of Crete."

I managed a tight smile. "That's true."

The policeman nodded, then walked past me and pushed through another set of doors.

He was gone.

A cold, sweet relief flooded through me. I sat perfectly still, breathing slowly to bring my pulse back to normal.

But to no avail. Even without the police involved, I still didn't feel safe. So much had happened so quickly, it wasn't possible to keep up with all the developments.

I thought of everyone who'd been at Christos' house, and the things they might have seen or overheard. Maybe someone other than Yaya had noticed the oil. Perhaps after the initial drama had faded, questions would be asked.

And Christos wasn't dead yet. He could still wake up and talk about what had happened. If Yaya or anyone else mentioned the oil, Christos might be able to connect the dots and realize what I had done.

I wasn't safe yet. And neither was Aspasia.

As promised, Aunt Hara produced relatives. I had been alone with Christos about two hours when cousins charged through the door, laden with food and deep concern.

More relatives came in the early evening, and they insisted I go home to my daughter. A different set of cousins would come to spend the night, and Aunt Hara and I would return in the morning to relieve them. Usually it was the very closest relatives who took the night shift, but with Dimitris gone and his sisters unwilling to help, we were fortunate that Christos' extended family was prepared to step in.

I kept my expression grave as I hugged everyone goodbye, but in truth I was overjoyed to be leaving. I went out the door and hurried down the pale-green hallway.

As I rounded the corner, I nearly knocked down the unhealthy doctor, who was lurking near the nurses' station.

"Any change?" he asked.

"None that I can see."

"That's not very promising." He shrugged. "On the other hand, your father-in-law might wake up tomorrow."

"Let's hope," I said, trying to look sincere.

He patted me on the shoulder. "You've done your duty for today."

"Yes," I agreed. "I certainly have."

As I drove back to the village, my thoughts turned to former President Bush.

I had never been particularly interested in politics, but as I navigated the twisting roads, he suddenly came to mind. I remembered the famous story of Bush weighing his options after Saddam Hussein invaded Kuwait in 1990. That was when Margaret Thatcher famously told him, "Remember, George, this is no time to go wobbly."

And so it was with me. This was no time to go wobbly.

Next Two Weeks

Once the shock of Christos' accident had passed, our days fell into a new pattern.

After walking Aspasia to school, I collected Aunt Hara and drove to the hospital. We stayed until two in the afternoon, then returned to the village. I didn't have to cancel a single class, which meant no loss of income for me and no loss of progress for my students.

Yaya picked up Aspasia from school every day and brought her over to Aunt Hara's house. The two of them got along famously. It was good for Yaya to spend her time doing something other than arguing with Aunt Hara, and each day Aspasia handed me crooked pieces of crocheting that I praised to the skies.

Aspasia also helped Yaya bake cakes and cookies, as well as spinach and cheese pies. I took their homemade treats to the hospital, which made me extremely popular with the ancient-name family, not to mention the unhealthy doctor and nursing staff.

As the days passed, the hospital became our second home. We found out which café had the best coffee, where to buy magazines, and which doctors to trust. In addition to the icons and *mati* charms, Christos' side of the room was now filled with a backgammon board, a stack of magazines, and a small radio.

Our group had merged seamlessly with the ancient-name family. In the mornings when Aunt Hara and I arrived, we usually found Elektra engrossed in conversation with one of our cousins. I had developed a warm friendship with Clytemnestra, and although Aunt Hara would never admit it, she had struck up a flirtation with Pericles, who had also lost his spouse some years before. He praised Aunt Hara's cooking and her resemblance to Aliki Vougiouklaki, and she oohed and aahed over his years of travel and devotion to his father.

Aunt Hara's friendship with Pericles proved particularly useful whenever Christos soiled the sheets. A noise or smell would alert us to the problem, whereupon Pericles tapped Leonidas on the shoulder, and the two of them rolled Christos on his side and got to work. Wiping Christos' bottom was nobody's favorite task, but Pericles did it every time without complaint.

"You should marry Pericles," I told Aunt Hara one day as we drove back to the village. "He's kind and he's still handsome. Plus he adores you."

"Get married again? Bah, never." But I could tell the idea pleased her.

Non-Greeks would surely have been shocked at the sight of eight or more people eating, laughing, and discussing *Lampsi* in the same room as two comatose men. Sometimes Aunt Hara and I felt guilty about enjoying ourselves, but as Clytemnestra observed one day, "It would be different if my father and your poor man were suffering. For all we know, they're already in heaven with Christ and Mary and all the saints. Maybe they're the ones crying for us."

Her father's eyes, however, were closed. Christos' open eye remained as it was, a veiny orb staring coldly into space.

No one else commented on the eye. Apparently I was the only one bothered by it. Once I cornered the unhealthy doctor and asked if he could close the lid. He shrugged and said he would try, but nothing ever changed. I was never alone with Christos, so I had no opportunity to simply close it myself.

How I hated that eye! It was a bleak reminder that Christos was not yet dead. He could still wake up and tell everyone he had no idea why there was olive oil in his shower base. Since he had showered the day before with no problem, someone must have put the oil there at some point on Sunday. I was the only person who came to his house that day, therefore it must have been me.

Those thoughts tortured me. Sometimes I woke up in the middle of the night, my heart beating in my head and my mouth dry as sand. It wasn't guilt that haunted me, rather it was fear. The horror of losing my family and my freedom, the threat of being exposed as an attempted murderer.

The only thing that eased my panic was company and lots of it. Mornings were the hospital, afternoons English classes, and evenings were for Aspasia. I dreaded the moment when she went to sleep and I no longer had any distractions to cover up my terror.

I had never regretted giving up drinking, but it certainly would have been a relief during those nightmare days. I asked the unhealthy doctor for a mild sedative, and he gave me a prescription without asking a single question. Aspasia was still sleeping in my bed, and the moment her eyes closed, I popped a pill in my mouth and read until my eyelids eased shut. Often in the mornings, Aspasia had to shake my arm to wake me from my stupor.

It was all part of the new pattern, the rearrangement of our lives around the still point of Christos lying unconscious in the hospital bed. We stayed beside him while he teetered on the edge of life and death, all of us waiting for that mute body to make a choice—to shut down completely or to rise up once more.

Yaya kept mentioning the olive oil. She just couldn't let it go.

Her comments always came out of nowhere. In the middle of cleaning a pile of sesame seeds or packing up cake for the hospital, Yaya would raise her head and say, "Why did Christos have oil in there? Why?"

Ignoring Yaya's questions was not an option. Instead we had long discussions where we listed all the possible reasons one might have olive oil in the bathroom. Did Christos like to rub his sore shoulder with the oil? Maybe he massaged it into his hair. Or perhaps he was using it as a moisturizer.

None of these theories satisfied Yaya.

"Christos was not a stupid man," she insisted. "He had to know it was a dangerous thing to do. I would never let oil spill on the floor in any room of my house, unless I was rubbing it into wood. Even then I'd be sure to put down a towel to soak up the drops."

"True," I agreed.

"It's also odd that there wasn't a bottle or dish with oil in the room. Did Christos bring in a handful himself?"

"Maybe."

"It would be difficult opening the door with olive oil cupped in his hands."

"Good point."

Fortunately Yaya never mentioned the possibility of murder. Not yet, anyway.

Yaya had also taken to discussing the oil with Aunt Hara. Luckily Aunt Hara seemed completely uninterested. It was just another one of Yaya's fixations that she tried to tune out.

Still, I wished Aunt Hara didn't know. And I longed for Yaya to drop the whole thing. The paranoia I felt was slowly unraveling me.

Like the day I left the hospital room to buy coffee, and I came back to find the room pregnant with a peculiar silence. Aunt Hara's expression was closed, and she replied to all my comments in a cold monotone.

I became suddenly and unshakably convinced that everyone knew the truth. Maybe Aspasia had confided in Yaya about what happened, and Yaya told Aunt Hara. When Aunt Hara mentioned the mystery of the oil to the ancient-name family, one of them wondered if someone had poured the oil deliberately, with the hope of harming Christos.

"But who?" they asked Aunt Hara. "Is there someone who wants to hurt him?"

That's when things clicked for Aunt Hara. She suddenly understood why I had asked so many questions about Eleni, and she realized that the person who wanted to hurt Christos was me.

They know, I thought, my hand trembling as I lifted the coffee cup to my lips. Now they're waiting for my nerves to snap. Or for Christos to wake up and tell them everything.

The following hours felt like torture. Each glance was an accusation, every sentence a double entendre. When Leonidas asked me if he had put enough olive oil on the salad, I almost bit my tongue in half.

As Aunt Hara and I got into the car to drive back to the village, I steeled myself for a confrontation. She was too conscious of public opinion to accuse me in front of the others, but nothing would stop her once we were on our own.

After ten minutes of silence, Aunt Hara cleared her throat. "We had an interesting discussion while you were out buying coffee."

"Is that so?" I replied, trying to keep my voice level.

"We were talking about their cousin who's getting married. That's when Pericles said he hated living alone and would love to have a wife again."

"Really."

"Then he looked at me and just stared. Everyone else was smiling, like they'd already talked about Pericles and me. I was so embarrassed!"

"So that's what happened," I said as casually as I could. "There was definitely a funny feeling in the room."

Aunt Hara shuddered. "It was such an awkward moment. You know how it is when someone says one thing, but everyone knows they mean something else."

"Yes," I agreed. "It's excruciating."

That hysterical laughter bubbled up again, and once more I forced it down.

I was safe after all. But for how long?

I almost fainted one morning when the door to Christos' room opened and Haralambis strolled in, Retsina at his heels.

Oh God, I thought. What does he want? I hadn't seen him since the dinner at my house, and I had no idea if he suspected anything.

The ancient-name family was intrigued by this handsome new arrival. Aunt Hara linked arms with Haralambis and proudly introduced him to our new friends.

While Aunt Hara beamed at his side, Haralambis said he had come to pay his respects and see if we needed any help. Pericles asked how he managed to get a dog into the hospital, and Haralambis said he told the unhealthy doctor that Retsina was Christos' dog. The plan was for Retsina to bring Christos out of his coma, just like a little boy in America who woke up when his dog licked him. The unhealthy doctor agreed it was worth a try, and Retsina was issued a special pass.

The ancient-name family praised Haralambis for his ingenuity. A few minutes later, he was seated between Elektra and Clytemnestra with a full plate of food, and Retsina was in the corner gnawing on a pork chop. Just one big happy family.

Except for me. As my anxiety mounted, I kept a brittle smile on my face. When Haralambis and Aunt Hara started discussing their puzzlement over Christos' accident, I stood up and volunteered to go buy coffee.

Haralambis decided to come with me. On the way to the café, I babbled nervously, filling him in on the ancient-name family and Aunt Hara's new romance. While we were waiting in line for our drinks, Haralambis took my wrist and fixed me with his special stare.

"Forget about all of them," he said. "How are you?"

"What do you mean?"

"This must be hard on you, with Dimitris so far away."

"It's not too bad," I said, my tone neutral. "We have lots of company, as you can see. And Christos isn't in pain. That's something to be thankful for."

Haralambis rubbed his handsome jaw. "Christos wouldn't be too happy if he knew I was here. Tell me, does Dimitris know yet?"

"We haven't told him. The doctor said—and Aunt Hara and I agree—that since Dimitris can't do anything to help out, there's no point worrying him. And Christos might still wake up."

"That wouldn't surprise me," Haralambis commented. "The old bastard is strong as a donkey. That eye is pretty unnerving though, eh?"

I looked away, pretending to watch the woman filling our order.

"What about Aspasia?" he asked. "How is she?"

"Fine. For the most part."

"She must be upset. I think she's the only person I ever saw Christos be kind to."

"Aspasia's with Yaya now. They've gotten quite close."

"Lucky kid."

"Yes, she is."

We brought the coffee back to the hospital room. With Retsina fast asleep at his feet, Haralambis entertained everyone with charming stories about growing up in our village. To my relief, there were no questions from him about flies in the wine, or olive oil in the shower base.

Not yet, anyway.

Monday

On a Monday, exactly two weeks after Christos fell, Sophia came to the hospital for the first time.

Her haughty dignity threatened to dampen the festivities. At least until Leonidas called her "mademoiselle" and complimented her on every aspect of her appearance until she was blushing and giggling. Finally Sophia consented to try Elektra's spinach pies, and with that she became one of us.

Sophia was halfway through a piece of Clytemnestra's yellow cake when she clicked her tongue and put down her fork.

"Katerina, I forgot to tell you. The postman gave me a letter for you from Dimitris. It's here, in my purse."

She reached into a black leather bag that was more luggage than purse, rummaging around until she produced a battered airmail envelope.

My heart jumped. Dimitris! At last.

I excused myself and went to sit on the bench in the pale-green hallway. The letter said, in Greek:

Katerina my love,

Finally we are in Japan! After we left Singapore, I could think of nothing but how it would feel to touch land again. Now that I'm here, I realize it's not any land I want, it's Crete. I keep thinking about what Kazantzakis wrote: "If it were possible to be born again, I would like to once again see the light here in these lands. There is an irresistible magic here." In other words, I'm much too old for all this traveling.

I was so happy to pick up your letters at the shipping company's office. Especially the pictures of you and Aspasia. I can't believe how much she's grown in just four months!

I miss you both terribly.

Your new class for the younger children is a great idea, and it's smart to make the lessons seem like playing. But I think you could include Aspasia. If you speak to her about not being bossy, I'm sure she'll be fine. Which may be naive of me, but if Aspasia wants to join in, it wouldn't hurt to try.

I'm glad to hear that everything is working out with Eleni. Do you ever sit and talk with her, or do you just leave the food and go? I hope you can chat a bit. And why not bring Aspasia along sometime? I know Eleni would love to see her.

You seem fine but a little lonely. I'm lonely too. The other crew members have gone off to find girlfriends for the week, so I hardly see them. Thankfully there's a Greek restaurant near the port. The owner is a man named Nikos who used to travel on cargo ships, but then he married a Japanese woman and settled here. He speaks fluent Japanese, which is funny to hear out of a big Greek man with tattoos on his arms.

Nikos has four beautiful children, and one girl is Aspasia's age. She looks more Japanese than Greek, but she still reminds me of Aspasia. We've become friends, and Nikos encourages me to speak Greek to her since he wants his children to learn Greek as well as Japanese and English.

He also told me about a few other Greek restaurants, and I've eaten in all of them. Everyone is happy to see me and talk about Greece. Sometimes that helps, but sometimes it makes me more homesick than ever.

I don't mean to sound sad. I'm doing fine, it's just that of course I'd rather be with you. Only five months left! I'm almost half done, and by now I've earned quite a bit of money for your new school. I have to keep reminding myself that's the reason we're doing all this!

In three weeks or so, we'll be in San Diego. It would be nice if we were stopping in Hawaii, but we're not. I'll read your letters again to get me through, and since my cabin is covered in pictures of you and Aspasia, I feel you're always close to me.

Greetings to everyone! Tell Aunt Hara and Yaya I sent them a letter from Singapore, they should have it by now. I also wrote to Eleni and Haralambis. From what you said, it seems you don't see him much. Please invite him for dinner, you know that our family is the only stable thing in his life other than Retsina.

I send you kisses and lots of love.
Dimitris

There was another letter in the envelope, written in big letters:

Aspasia my love,

How is my favorite girl in the whole world? I miss you very much, and I think about you all the time. I imagine you at school, at home, playing with your cats, in the *kafenio* with your *papoos*.

I am in Japan now. Japan is an island like Crete, but with more people and no olive trees. I have a friend here, a Greek man who has a restaurant. His wife is Japanese and they have a little girl who's your age. She speaks Japanese and English and a little Greek. You would like her.

I love you very much, and I can't wait until I see you again. And guess what? I bought you a doll here, so now you have dolls from Holland, Belgium, Senegal, South Africa, Madagascar, India, Singapore, and Japan!

Please be good and do as your mommy says.

Many kisses,

Your daddy

I didn't have a tissue, so I wiped my eyes with my sleeve. Dimitris was living in a time warp, a world innocent of Aspasia's rape and my attempt to murder his father. A safe space, without the open staring eye. If only I could grab Aspasia and climb into that fantasy world with him!

All this time, I had been clinging to the idea of asking Dimitris to come home once he arrived in San Diego. After reading his letters, I decided not to. I preferred him to remain as he was, blissfully innocent and wonderfully whole.

At least for now.

I had just started to reread the letters when the door to Christos' room flew open. Aunt Hara rushed out, her face white and her hands waving frantically.

"Go find the doctor! Now!"

"What's going on?"

"Christos is waking up!"

Fingers shaking, I tucked the letters in my sweater pocket. The moment was finally here. Christos was conscious, and I had to face him.

This was no time to go wobbly.

"Hurry!" Aunt Hara yelled, then disappeared back into the room.

I rushed down the hallway, looking for the doctor as I ran. A nurse told me she had seen him leave, an orderly said he had come back, and another doctor thought he was in the bathroom.

Finally I tracked him down in the lobby, talking to a pretty nurse beside the water fountain.

"Come quickly!" I commanded. "My father-in-law is waking up."

We went up two flights of stairs and down the long hallway. The doctor was so slow I had to grab his wrist and pull him.

When we burst through the door, everyone was standing and looking at Christos. His whole body was jerking up and down, a gurgling sound erupting from his open mouth.

The doctor went up to Christos and put a hand on his chest. Turning to me and Aunt Hara, he said, "You misunderstood. He's not waking up. He's dying."

The gurgling and convulsing continued for another thirty minutes. Christos wasn't going to give up easily.

Sophia and the ancient-name family stepped discreetly into the hallway, leaving me, Aunt Hara, and two female cousins alone with the doctor and Christos. I held Aunt Hara's hand as she dabbed her eyes with a tissue, and together we watched and waited.

I kept my expression mournful, hiding the surge of elation rising in my chest. My nightmare was almost over.

Suddenly, Christos arched his back. He exhaled with a deep, eerie moan, and his body collapsed.

The doctor put on his stethoscope and held the flat end to Christos' chest. He listened for a full minute, then took the stethoscope out of his ears and put it back around his neck.

"He's dead," the doctor announced.

The eye, however, was still open.

After Christos was pronounced dead, the doctor tried to close the open eye. Without success. Finally he gave up and drew a sheet over Christos' head.

Aunt Hara and I signed a slew of papers, then we cleaned up our side of the hospital room. We said a tearful goodbye to the ancient-name family, accompanied by affectionate cheek kisses and a final wistful glance between Pericles and Aunt Hara.

A hearse brought Christos' corpse back to the village, and the coffin was set up in the middle of Christos' living room for the all-night vigil. The funeral would be the next day, as was customary in Greece.

While Yaya and a few other women from the village busied themselves in the kitchen, Aunt Hara and I opened the windows and swept out the dust. Being in Christos' house unnerved me. I couldn't stop looking in the bathroom, as if I were afraid the image of me pouring oil into the shower base was burned into the room forever. But the bathroom was spotless, its history thankfully silent.

Finally the priest arrived. I smelt *raki* on his breath as he kissed me on the cheeks and murmured a few words about God's grace and Christos' importance in the community. I longed to ask how decades of incest, pedophilia, and physical violence could be considered important, but instead I put on a sad expression and nodded.

The priest's wife wasn't far behind. She came in clucking sympathy and bearing a plate of cookies. I never liked her; she had cunning eyes and a sarcastic sense of humor. Somehow I managed to smile at her and murmur a few polite nothings. She patted my cheek and went to speak to Aunt Hara.

After one of the women served him some food, the priest stationed himself by the coffin. Incense, chanting, and the sound of clicking beads filled the house.

Aunt Hara and another woman made coffee, then we sat on the couch and quietly discussed who to notify. Stamatina, of course, and other relatives in Athens and Thessaloniki. A telegram to Dimitris via the shipping company, and letters from Aunt Hara to our relatives in America and Australia.

Somebody also needed to speak to Eleni. Sophia had driven to Eleni's house several times to drop off food and update her on Christos' health, but Eleni had refused to be on the rotating squad of hospital visitors. A few people grumbled about that, although no one really expected anything different.

Not surprisingly, I was elected to go to Eleni's house to break the news of Christos' death. I was also expected to drag her back to the village so she could mourn with the rest of us.

"She won't come," I told them.

"You have to try," Aunt Hara pleaded. "This one time, Eleni needs to be here."

"He was her father," the priest's wife chimed in. "It would be a sin not to sit with him."

"Eleni won't come," I repeated. "I'll talk to her, but I doubt it will do any good."

"Go now," the priest's wife ordered. "And when you're back, bring Aspasia too."

"She won't be coming either."

"What do you mean?"

"Aspasia's too young. She'll be scared."

I couldn't tell them the truth, namely that Christos didn't deserve a farewell from Aspasia, and I was damned if he was going to get one.

"Zucchinis!" the priest's wife said. "She was Christos' favorite, you must bring her."

"I don't think young children should look at corpses. That's not how we do things in America," I lied.

"You're not in America now."

I looked her in the eye. "Aspasia is my daughter, and that's what I've decided."

The priest's wife crossed herself and exchanged glances with the other women. I knew what those looks meant. They were reminding each other that I was a foreigner and not a member of the Greek Orthodox church, and therefore I didn't have a clue.

A battle ensued. I had lived in Crete long enough to know that the secret to arguing with a Greek was to yell loudly, wave your hands wildly, and never budge from your position. So I shouted at the priest's wife, and she shouted at me. The priest glanced over at us several times, but one look at his cowering face told me who was the boss in that marriage.

When the priest's wife realized I wasn't going to yield, she shrugged and said in a quieter voice, "As you like. But can you at least stop at your house and change into mourning clothes?"

"Of course," I said tersely.

As I put on my coat, still trembling after all the screaming, I wondered what would happen if I didn't come back at all. Or if I appeared in my favorite spring dress, blue with big yellow flowers, ready to dance all night to celebrate the death of an evil man.

Yaya walked me home so she could pick up her sewing basket.

"Good for you," she said when we were out of earshot. "When I was Aspasia's age, my mother made me kiss a corpse. I never forgot it."

"I'm glad you understand."

Yaya walked gingerly along the cobblestone street. "You have mourning clothes, right? I remember you wore them to Pepina's funeral."

"I have plenty. Most of my wardrobe was black when I came here, that's all I ever wore in New York."

Yaya nodded. "I remember. Aunt Hara and I thought that was very strange."

I laughed. "I'm sure you did."

"You can always borrow something of mine."

I put my arm around her. "Yaya, I could fit you in my pocket if I wanted to. I don't think I can wear your clothes."

She patted my hand. "By the way," she said. "I figured it out."

"What?"

"The olive oil. I know why it was there."

Red crackled before my eyes. Here it comes, I thought. "And why is that?"

"Not now. We can talk after the funeral."

My legs shook so hard I had trouble walking. Even if Yaya had somehow figured out I was the one who put the oil in the shower, it didn't mean she was going to tell anyone.

Or did it?

I couldn't be sure. But there was one thing I did know. This was no time to go wobbly.

Mrs. D was on sentry duty. When she saw Yaya and me approaching, she actually rose up off her bench.

"Such a pity!" she cried out, gripping my hands as Yaya ran inside the house. "A man in his prime dying like that! I'll come to the vigil, of course. I'm making *pastitsio* now."

"Thank you," I replied. "That's very kind of you."

"It's ironic about the house, isn't it?"

"What do you mean?"

"Christos' house is yours now. You can use it for your school. Dimitris didn't need to go away after all, did he?"

I blinked. I hadn't thought about that, but of course Mrs. D was right. Stamatina and Eleni wouldn't want the house, so now it was ours. But there was no way I was going to set up my school in the house where Aspasia had been attacked.

"You go on inside," Mrs. D said. "I'm sure you have so much to do. Remember I'm here if you need me."

I found an old black skirt and shirt, but I had nothing to wear over them. Yaya and I went back to her house, where I selected one of Aunt Hara's extensive collection of black sweaters.

Afterward Yaya went back to the vigil, and I stopped at Despina's to speak to Aspasia. She had cried when Yaya told her the news, and I wanted to make sure she was all right.

Despina's mother said the girls were playing in the back room. I peeked through the doorway and saw them engrossed with their dolls. Aspasia looked fine, so I decided not to disturb her by sweeping in like a crow in my black clothes. I thanked Despina's mother for keeping Aspasia, and she said it was no problem.

"When do you want me to send Aspasia home?" she asked.

In Greece, children didn't typically have sleepovers like they did in America. But I really needed some time to myself.

"Do you mind if she stays overnight?" I asked. "I'll pick her up tomorrow after the funeral."

"Aspasia won't be paying last respects to her *papoos*?"

"In America, we never let children see corpses or go to funerals," I lied. "That's how I was brought up."

"Didn't she go to her grandmother Pepina's funeral?"

People here never forgot anything! "Aspasia was younger then. She didn't understand."

Despina's mother nodded, although I could tell she didn't approve. And why should she, why should anyone? The gossip mill was certainly going to have a good time with this one.

Let them talk, I thought. I know what I'm doing.

As I drove out of the village, rain started splashing on the windshield. I went slowly, partly to avoid tumbling down the mountainside, but mostly because I wasn't eager to rush back to the vigil.

I entered the riverbed and parked in the gorge under Eleni's house. She came outside holding an umbrella, Platon the dog at her heels.

"Hurry!" she called. "You'll get soaked."

I raced up the steep path and went into the kitchen. A saucepan of water and sage leaves was bubbling on the stove, and a book was facedown on the table.

Eleni shook out her umbrella in the open doorway, then closed the door. She leaned against the wall and stared at me as I took off my coat and smoothed down my hair.

"So he's dead," she said.

"Yes. How did you—?"

"Your clothes."

"I came here to tell you."

"And bring me back so I can do my duty as a daughter and sit with my father's corpse."

"Something like that."

"I'm not going." Eleni's hand shook as she poured sage tea into two cups. "If my husband were here, he'd understand."

"I agree with you," I said quietly. "Don't come."

She tilted her head. "I'm surprised to hear you say that. You're the perfect daughter-in-law. I think you're more Greek than I am."

"I don't know about that."

Eleni brought the teacups to the table, and we drank in silence.

I had thought that Eleni was completely different from me, but she was not. Her misfortune was that she still lived in the place where she had unleashed her howling pain and anger, whereas I had put an ocean between myself and the past. The old Katerina—Katherine—was completely unknown here, while the old Eleni roamed in the memory of every villager.

Then I remembered Eleni's husband, with his stutter, plain face, and gentle manner. What a shame he had died so young.

"I agree with you," I said, louder now. "Don't go. And I'm sorry if you ever thought I intended to convince you."

Eleni knit her brows. "You mean that?"

"I do."

She put down her cup and stared at me. "I believe you," she said finally.

We sat in silence for a while, then she rose and brought over a chocolate bar. As I watched Eleni break the chocolate into squares, I decided that one day soon, I would tell her everything. Not about the murder, because I planned to take that secret to my grave. But I would let her know what Christos had done to Aspasia. Eleni's heart was big enough to hold that truth.

I would wait until after the funeral to tell her. Then I would bring Aspasia here so she could get to know her aunt. They had a lot in common, both light and shadow.

Tuesday

The funeral passed in a blur for me. The crowded church was heavy with incense, sobbing, and the priest's droning voice. I put a sad expression on my face and endured everyone's sympathy.

The gathering afterward at Christos' house was just as hazy. I stood among the villagers crammed inside the little house, the air dense with loud talk and cigarette smoke, everyone pressing in around the tables for food, wine, and *raki*.

I just wanted the day to end so I could hear what Yaya had to say about the oil. My fear came in waves, but I managed to hold myself together, due mostly to swigging coffee and stuffing my face with sweets. When Yaya finally told me she was ready to leave, I put my arm around her and led her out the door.

It was raining that day as well. Just a gentle drizzle, so we didn't bother with umbrellas. I linked arms with Yaya so she wouldn't fall, though it felt like she was the one holding me up.

The moment we were on our own, I looked Yaya in the eye. "Tell me about the olive oil."

Yaya grimaced. "It's unpleasant."

"Go ahead. I can take it."

"Christos was—you know."

"I don't know. What?"

"He was playing with himself. Like men do."

I blinked. "That's what you figured out?"

Yaya nodded wisely. "Christos was old, so maybe you think he didn't do things like that anymore. But until the day she died, he was coming after Pepina. I know because she told me."

My stomach twisted in disgust. "But Pepina was so ill! She could hardly walk."

"That didn't stop him."

I bit my lip. Christos' sex life was the last thing I wanted to discuss.

But—that was it? Yaya didn't suspect me? No police, no jail, no public disgrace? No desperate pleading with her to keep my secret?

I folded my arms around Yaya and laid my cheek on top of her head. The tears came then, a flood of relief as I let go of the barbwire of tension that had been torturing me for weeks. In the middle of the village, I cried long and loud while Yaya held on to me with her thin, strong arms.

A few villagers passed by just then. "*Ela*," I heard one of the men say. "See how much Christos' daughter-in-law loved him."

Five Months Later

In May, Crete explodes with flowers. Red and white and purple, pink and blue and yellow. It's my favorite month of the year.

On a warm Saturday afternoon, I took Aspasia on a picnic to our favorite pine grove in the mountains. The magic spot, she called it.

I spread a blanket over the needle-covered ground. We ate hard-boiled eggs, fish roe salad, sliced tomatoes, fresh bread, and chocolate bars. Afterward I sat on the blanket with my hands wrapped around my knees, watching as Aspasia collected flowers.

"Look, Mommy!" She dropped a colorful tangle onto the blanket. "Can you help me put them in bunches?"

We sorted by color, then made bouquets for Aunt Hara, Yaya, and her Aunt Eleni.

"Honey," I said when we were done. "I'd like to talk to you about something."

"OK," she said. "What?"

Aspasia sat on my outstretched legs, facing me with her small, serious face. Her hair was parted on the side and held in place by a small pink barrette. She was wearing her favorite flower-patterned smock, along with the jeans I had bought for her at the outdoor market in Sitia.

I cleared my throat. "First I want to say I'm sorry, because I don't think I've been a good mommy these past months. You've been spending lots of time with Yaya and Despina, but not really with me."

Aspasia curled her lips in and out, which meant I was right.

"I'm sorry," I told her. "Everything just felt so weird after your *papoos* died."

The giddy joy I felt after Christos' death and burial had lasted a few days. When the relief subsided, reality crept in. I had erased Christos from the earth, but I could never change what he had done to Aspasia. It was impossible to prevent the aftershocks that kept spreading throughout my family's life.

The bitter truth was that Aspasia was not the same little girl she had been just half a year before. She cried easily for no reason, and she was afraid to go outside on her own. Sometimes she got furiously angry, even hitting Despina several times. And once when I walked into Aspasia's room unannounced, I found her masturbating. Not that she even understood what she was doing; it was undoubtedly a reaction to being exposed to sex at such a young age.

But Aspasia was my daughter. And what happened with her *papoos* was not her fault. Even though she had lost her innocence, she was still innocent.

"We won't live like that anymore," I promised.

"OK."

"So tell me. How did you feel after your *papoos* died?"

Aspasia twisted her lips. "Sad. But not really."

"Because of what he did to you?"

She nodded.

Go on, I told myself. "And when you think about what your *papoos* did to you, how do you feel?"

Her eyes filled with tears. "I feel really bad."

I grabbed her in my arms. She lay her head on my chest and cried.

When the tears were all out and she could finally speak, Aspasia sputtered, "He should not have did that, Mommy. I'm glad he's dead." She looked up at me, mucus blowing in and out of her nostrils. "But that's bad to say."

"No, it's not," I assured her. "Because I'm glad he's dead too. He had no right to attack you the way he did."

"Where is he now?"

"Who?"

"*Papoos*."

"Why, he's dead. He's buried in the ground."

She looked doubtful.

"Aspasia, you know he's dead. He can't hurt you anymore."

"What about his ghost?"

"His ghost! Is that why you're still afraid to go out?"

She knit her brows. "It's not that I've seen him. But Despina said he was here."

"How does she know something like that?"

"Her *yaya* said that ghosts stay in the place where they lived when they were people. Despina said *papoos* is still here in the village."

I thought a moment. "Is that why you hit Despina?"

Aspasia tightened her lips and nodded.

I moved her back a little and made sure she was looking me in the eye. "Listen. I know for a fact that Christos' ghost isn't here."

"How come?"

"Because ghosts don't always stay where they lived. Despina's wrong. Ghosts can travel anywhere they want without paying for plane tickets. Why would your *papoos* want to stay around here?"

Aspasia considered this. "So his ghost isn't waiting for me?"

"Nope. It's probably visiting Australia, or maybe Antarctica."

"Or his ghost traveled back in time, and now it's living in the Wild West."

"Could be," I laughed. "He always did like cowboy movies."

"I bet that's where *papoos* is," Aspasia said with relief. "He's somewhere riding a horse."

I stroked her hair.

"I miss Daddy," she said suddenly.

"Me too," I replied sadly. "But just two more weeks and he'll be home. We can manage until then, don't you think?"

"I guess so."

I kissed her again. Now that she was calm, I told her I loved her, and so did her daddy, Aunt Hara, Yaya, her Aunt Eleni, and all her friends. I said that the life was indeed comfortable, but people like her *papoos* didn't know that, so they made problems for others.

"I also want you to know that whenever you need to talk about your *papoos* and what happened, you can always come to me. And we'll tell your daddy everything when he gets home. All right?"

"OK. Can I go pick more flowers?"

Of course. I let her go and watched as she ran out of the pine grove.

I felt a little better, although I still had so much ahead of me.

The biggest challenge would be telling Dimitris what had happened. I imagined him walking through the door, throwing down his duffel bag, and grabbing Aspasia and me into his arms. Not to mention the happy chatter from our fellow villagers, who would be hanging around outside our house to welcome him back. What joy to be home after traveling so long!

There would be no need to tell Dimitris right away. I would let him enjoy his homecoming. For a week at least, maybe more. But the day would come when I would have to sit him down for a serious talk.

I had already decided not to discuss what I did to Christos. Confessing my secret wouldn't absolve me; it would merely shift the burden onto Dimitris too.

Another reason I didn't want to tell him was because I was worried about his reaction. Dimitris would most likely understand why I had killed his father. But it was possible he would be deeply shocked, and then he would never see me the same way again. That was something I couldn't bear.

I did, however, need to tell Dimitris what Christos had done to Aspasia. And when I told him, I would have to watch his face fill with horror and see all the joy fade from his eyes.

That alone was bad enough. But how long before Dimitris understood what I had already realized, that the Aspasia we once knew was gone forever?

God damn that bastard Christos! How I wished he were still alive, just so I could have the exquisite pleasure of murdering him again.

THE END

Afterword

From November 1990 to August 1995, I lived in a small fishing village in Crete. It was during those years that I wrote *Aspasia*.

The novel was motivated by two very different Greek stories. The first was the book *Astradeni* by Eugenia Fakinou, about a young girl who moves from a Greek island to Athens. In the last paragraph of the book, Astradeni is sexually molested by a neighbor. I liked the book but found the ending extremely dark, and I wanted to write a book where a young girl facing a similar situation was protected.

The second was Sophocles' play *Antigone*, which explores the clash between personal conscience and the law, namely when Antigone defies the king to do what she believes is right.

Another motivation for *Aspasia* was a conversation with a Cretan friend. She and her mother were discussing a news story about a Greek girl who was sexually molested by a relative, and my friend's mother said, "Oh, that happened in my village all the time." I wondered about those children, and I thought about how they could have been protected. Or perhaps how they were protected.

At the time I wrote *Aspasia*, I had a literary agent in New York who appreciated my work and had tried to sell three of my novels. My agent did not, however, like *Aspasia*. She had no problem with the writing, but she disliked the subject matter and declined to represent the book.

My agent's refusal was a painful blow, but I still believed in *Aspasia*. When technology made self-publishing a sensible alternative, I published the book with iUniverse in 2003. Because *Aspasia* is short, I combined it with another novel I wrote about Crete called *Mrs. Papadakis*. I gave the book the rather unwieldy title *Mrs. Papadakis and Aspasia: Two Novels*.

In the era before social media, the only way to get reviews was via newspapers and magazines, both physical and online. I did receive a few for *Mrs. Papadakis and Aspasia*, mostly positive, but neither novel ever truly took flight. Over the next twenty years, readers occasionally discovered the books, but overall they lived a quiet life on Amazon and other online booksellers.

As I write this in spring 2025, the publishing world is obviously much different, particularly the marketing aspect. I've had the good fortune of working with independent book reviewers on Instagram and other platforms, so this seemed like the right time to rerelease *Aspasia*.

I also think that the book's topic is no longer as taboo as it was in 1994. Although the description of the attack might be shocking, the fact that it occurred will presumably surprise very few.

The other difference is that I now have thirty more years of experience with writing, so hopefully I know a bit more about how to structure a book. I have done a deep edit of *Aspasia*, most notably taking away a lengthy back story that disturbed the narrative flow. The back story is alluded to several times in the current version, but I feel sure that the book is better off without it.

The timing is also good for a rerelease because, much to my surprise and delight, I have been spending time in Crete again after nearly three decades away. Crete has of course changed a great deal in that time, due mostly to the advent of computers and social media, so I'm glad this book brings a vanished world back to life.

On a final note, I hope that my Cretan family and friends will not be offended by the character of Christos Theodorakis. Unfortunately there are people like him in all countries, not just Greece. But there is a tradition in Greece—and indeed, Greek literature—of taking care of your family at all costs, and I hope Katerina's courage pays tribute to that legacy.

As for Aspasia, I imagine that she's grown up now with children of her own. I'm sure she does whatever she can to protect them, just as her mother once protected her.

I also imagine that one of Dimitris' shipmates comes to visit and falls madly in love with Eleni—and vice versa. If anyone deserves a happy ending, it's her.

Thank You

Carol Binkowski. Many thanks for your help with the back cover text, and for all our wonderful conversations about writing.

C. Fitton. Warm thanks for reading *Aspasia* and writing such a powerful cover blurb. Your support and positive outlook mean a great deal to me.

Daria Simanska. Ευχαριστώ for your help with Greek phrases, book marketing, and Cretan cookies. Your tireless enthusiasm for this project has been a gift.

Eleanor Huffman. I'm so grateful for our many enlightening conversations about Cretan customs. Your insights into the book's subject matter are also deeply appreciated.

Henry Chen. Heartfelt thanks for your beautiful cover design and artwork. I appreciate your creativity and meticulousness, as well as your steady patience.

Margarita Howard-Heretakis. Many thanks for reading *Aspasia* and offering, as always, insightful comments and warm encouragement.

Marilena Salamanou. Ευχαριστώ for your ideas about marketing and your love for Greek literature, which continues to inspire me.

Mihalis Heretakis. Ευχαριστώ for your steadfast support during the years when *Aspasia* was born.

Patricia Seminara. Your proofreading, thoughtful comments, and unrelenting support mean a great deal to me.

Stamatis Tsoumaris. Ευχαριστώ for your helpful tips on marketing books in Greece.

Tina Venetsanos. Ευχαριστώ for proofreading *Aspasia* and sharing valuable insights into Greek culture. I'm especially grateful for your help transliterating Greek words and our many discussions about writing.
.

Stay in Touch

Thank you so much for taking the time to read my book.

If you enjoyed *Aspasia: A Novel of Suspense and Secrets*, please consider leaving a review on one of the many available platforms, especially Amazon, Goodreads, and BookBub.

You can contact me at florencewetzel@yahoo.com. I'm on Facebook as Florence Wetzel, and Instagram as @florencewetzel108. You're also welcome to follow my author page on BookBub.

If you would like to join my email list to learn about my new releases, write to me at florencewetzel@yahoo.com.

Printed in Dunstable, United Kingdom